THE DOUBLE CROSSING

SYLVIA PATIENCE

copyright © 2023 by Sylvia Patience

All rights reserved.

No part of this book may be reproduced or transmitted in any form or by any means, electronic or mechanical, except for the purpose of review and/or reference, without explicit permission in writing from the publisher.

Cover design copyright © 2023 by Kelley York
sleepyfoxstudio.net

Published by Paper Angel Press
paperangelpress.com

ISBN 978-1-959804-22-2 (Trade Paperback)

10 9 8 7 6 5 4 3 2 1

FIRST EDITION

Acknowledgements

First, I'd like to thank my publisher Steven Radecki and his staff at Paper Angel Press for their support and for making it possible for the manuscript of *The Double Crossing* to become this book which you can read.

Sigrid Lonnberg read the manuscript, made suggestions, and corrected the German words and phrases in the book. She was a great friend and help to me.

Thanks to my critique groups for reading chapters week by week and giving me amazing, thoughtful suggestions. All my books are much better with their help. Thanks to Eric Hoffman, Carol Foote, Diane Landy, Jackie Pascoe, Eve Bunting, Carol Brendsel, Kate Bowland, Barbara Riverwoman, Louise Loots, and the others who've passed through the groups over the years I've been writing.

My family is my cheer squad, always supportive of my writing and promoting my books. Thanks to all of you.

The Double Crossing

Part One

1

HAMBURG
FRIDAY, MAY 12, 1939

HANNAH

THE BLACK BULK OF THE *ST. LOUIS* loomed several stories above the dock where I stood with Mother. Lifeboats and two mustard-colored funnels striped with red, white, and black caught my eye. Then I noticed something else red, white, and black. A swastika flag! It hung at the back of the ship, above the flag of the ship's owners, HAPAG, the Hamburg America Line. Gripping Mother's hand, I pointed.

"Look *Mutter*! It's a Nazi ship!"

"It doesn't mean anything Hannah, *Leibling*. All German ships must fly the Nazi flag." Mother stroked my hair. "Everything will be fine. You have your ticket, passport, and landing permit. Ruth will watch out for you."

Ruth! I hardly knew her. I was only thirteen and she was eighteen, the daughter of mother's friends from synagogue.

"But *Mutter*, I don't want to leave you. They could send you to a camp too."

"They won't, my love. They only took the men."

I wasn't sure. On *Kristallnacht*, the night of breaking glass, Nazis had destroyed Father's jewelry store and sent him, and all the Jewish men in Oldenburg, to a *Konzentrationslager*, a camp. Soon after, a Nazi officer took our home for himself. We had to move into a tiny apartment.

"I wish I could stay with you." Tears pressed behind my eyes. I was terrified of traveling to a new country and of what would happen to my mother, alone.

"*Vater* and I will join you when he comes home. Soon, I'm sure." Mother's face looked tired and broken.

"Promise you won't wait long? Even if he doesn't come."

"Of course, love," she said.

"*Mutter*, please, can't I get on the ship tomorrow? It doesn't leave until then."

"We talked about this," her voice began to sound impatient. "It's bad luck to begin a journey on the Sabbath. You need to be on board before the sun goes down."

I clenched my fists at my sides. Mother wasn't going to change her mind.

A few other passengers and their families waited on the quay, talking in low voices. Thuds of crates being loaded onto the ship, yells of workers, and squawking calls of gulls filled my ears like the chaos that filled my mind. My imagination, as usual, spun frightening stories—*ein Kopfkino*, like a movie in my head. The Nazis could take Mother away. Father might not come back. I'd be left in a strange country alone.

A faint stink of sewage from the river crept under the oil and diesel fumes. Mother coughed again, covering her mouth with her handkerchief. The smoke on the train had made her asthma worse. I should be here to take care of her.

Nearby, Ruth was hugging her parents. She was tall like her mother and wore a stylish suit. Her brown hair was waved and smooth, like mine never was. Next to her, I felt like a child, even wearing my best blue dress and with clips and bobby pins trying to tame my red curls. Mother always said my wild hair was like me, quick to fly out of control.

In a moment I'd have to say good-bye to Mother and climb the stairs to the ship's deck. I shivered.

Mother squeezed my hand. "Don't be afraid, my Hannah. Listen," she whispered, "I didn't want you to be nervous going through the customs shed, but I sewed two pairs of diamond earrings into the hem of your dress. Sell them in Cuba. It should be enough money for expenses until we get there."

I automatically reached down to feel the hem of my dress.

Mother took my hand. "Don't draw attention to it."

"Sorry, *Mutter*. Will you have enough money for you and *Vater* to make the trip?"

"You ask so many questions. Stop worrying. My jewelry will be enough. And surely your father will be home soon. Two more men just returned from the camp." She squeezed my hand. "I'm stronger than you think. I'll come to you, no matter what."

"*Mutter*, I love you. I'm so afraid!" I flung my arms around her thin shoulders.

"There, there." Mother patted my back. "Think how exciting it will be to sail across the ocean and see a new part of the world."

"I know." I sniffed and wiped my eyes. As far as I was concerned, the only good thing about going to Cuba would be to learn Spanish. I loved discovering new words, like when we studied English in school.

After everything Mother had done to get me out of Germany, I had to be brave.

Ruth tapped my shoulder. She smiled, her eyes sparkling with excitement. "Come on, Hannah. We'd better board the ship before sundown."

The Double Crossing

I looked up. The river glinted with the golden light of late afternoon. I swallowed and said, "I'm ready."

Mother kissed my cheek. "Go on. I'll see you soon. Before you know it."

"I love you, *Mutter*. Please come soon."

I tried to ignore the black cloud of dread hanging over me. So many things could go wrong. My mouth was dry. I had to wipe the slippery sweat from my hand with my skirt before I could pick up my suitcase.

Ruth took my other hand and pulled me after her. A few passengers were boarding early like us. Our footsteps rang on the metal stairs leading onto the ship.

When we reached the top, I turned to see Mother one last time. She waved. I took my hand from Ruth's to wave back. My heart felt like lead.

A young sailor reached for our suitcases and told us to follow him. We went down several flights of stairs. Our cabin was in tourist class, on the D deck. Ruth and the sailor talked the whole way. I didn't pay attention to what they said. After he left, Ruth shut the door and fell onto one of the beds. "What a dreamy guy. Do you think he was flirting with me?"

"I didn't notice." How could she think about boys at a time like this? I started to sit on the other bed, then I thought I should unpack my things. I put my suitcase on the bed but didn't open it. Maybe Mother was still on the quay and I could get one last look at her.

"I'm going back on the deck," I said.

"I'll go with you." Ruth bounced up. "We can look around. We might see that sailor again."

By the time we could see the quay, Mother and the Rubensteins, Ruth's parents, were gone. Probably heading to the train home already. I refused to cry again. I would be brave.

Ruth said, "Cheer up Hannah. Don't look so sad. Think of how much fun we'll have. There's going to be a swimming pool and all kinds of things to do. Let's explore."

"Not now." I wasn't interested in the ship or pools or adventures. "Tomorrow I'll go with you. All right?"

As Ruth went off to explore, maybe to find her sailor, I started back to the cabin to lie down. My head was full of fog. The ship was huge, so many decks and corridors. I hadn't paid attention and I got confused.

"You look lost. Can I help you?" A white-jacketed steward had seen me wandering. He seemed nice, but I didn't trust anyone who worked on this Nazi ship. And it was embarrassing to have to be shown the way to our cabin again.

I unpacked and changed out of my best dress, folding it neatly into the empty suitcase. I wouldn't wear it again. Not with diamonds in the hem. How do you sell diamonds anyway? I lay down on the bed, willing myself not to cry. I was on my own now.

I closed my eyes for a minute, and I was there again. *Kristallnacht* was six months ago, but it still repeated in my mind. Nazi storm troopers and thugs breaking windows, the smell of smoke and the red glow of flames from the burning synagogue, people screaming, dragged out and beaten. Father not coming back. I'd been so scared I'd thrown up.

I opened my eyes again to the cabin on the *St. Louis*, shaking my head to make those memories go away. Mother trusted me to do this. I'd show her I could.

2

HAMBURG
SATURDAY, MAY 13

DAVID

"THE SON OF A JEW and an Aryan is an abomination," the Director had said when he kicked me out of school with all the Jewish students. His ugly words stuck with me. I thought about them while we stood in the customs line watching Nazi inspectors shout rudely at passengers ahead of us.

"David and Rebekah let's be quiet and not attract attention," my father whispered to me and my sister. "These customs inspectors are not friendly."

The line wound through a huge shed that looked like a warehouse. Once we got past customs, we could board the ship to Cuba. The other passengers were mostly quiet and probably nervous like us, but the high shed roof echoed with shouted questions of the Nazi inspectors. They scowled and yelled while examining passports stamped with a red letter "J" for Jew, like ours. If they found something they didn't like, they could stop us from getting on the ship.

The Double Crossing

The smell of the Elbe River blew in from outside. Even though it stank a little of diesel and sewage, it reminded me of good times when Papa and I used to come down to the river to watch birds. I tried not to think about leaving our home in Hamburg to go live in a strange foreign country until Herr Hitler was gone.

Rebekah, my eight-year-old sister, held tight to our mother's hand. She whispered, "Mama, I'm scared."

"Don't worry, *Maus*. We'll be on the ship soon."

I thought Rebekah was getting big to be called mouse, but she was the youngest, the baby.

Papa reached over to smooth Rebekah's hair, his eyes still on the inspectors.

I was thirteen and not about to say I was scared. Even if maybe I was. I looked around at the other passengers. Some of them were traveling alone, mostly men. And some had shaved heads. Suddenly an inspector yelled at one of those men and a couple of guards dragged him out.

"Papa," I said into his ear, "What's happening? Why are they taking that man away? Why is his head shaved?"

Papa leaned close. "They shave men's heads in the camps. Now hush and don't say anything."

I knew about the concentration camps. Prisoners that came back told stories of lice and rats, of being starved and beaten, some people killed for no reason.

One of the men noticed me staring at him. I looked away quickly.

Finally, it was our turn. The inspector looked at us like we were bugs. I didn't think we had anything we weren't supposed to, but still … he could stop us from getting on the ship. He messed our things up, digging through our suitcases, tossing everything around.

All I had in my suitcase was my clothes and binoculars. When the inspector found Papa's binoculars and mine, he pulled them out. "What are you going to use these for?"

My heart just about fell into my stomach. Please, please don't take them.

"We're bird watchers," Papa said. "We hope to see new birds on the voyage, and in Cuba."

"Hmmph!" The officer held both pairs of binoculars in his hands, like he was weighing them. The Nazi party badge caught my eye, pinned to his uniform sleeve. "I'll let you keep them, but you'd better not watch anything besides birds. There are Gestapo on board and if they find you spying, you'll be brought back and severely punished."

"Yes, sir." Papa's face was red. I could see he was barely holding in his anger. I clenched my fists and didn't look at the inspector. So there were going to be Gestapo, Nazi secret police, on board the *St. Louis*.

At last we made it out of customs. None of our things had been taken. I could breathe again. We followed the crowd onto the quay. Rain had started falling while we were inside. The *St. Louis* towered before us, like a black and white cliff.

I tucked my hands in my jacket pockets and hunched my shoulders against the cold. A band under an awning played one of those oompah tunes. Passengers and their families and friends stood in a crowd, most wearing overcoats, and holding umbrellas. I saw a lot of other boys and girls boarding with their families. Maybe I'd make friends on the ship. At home the other boys had begun to stay away from me. They called me *schmutziger Jüde*, "dirty Jew," even though only my father was Jewish. And we weren't religious.

People hugged and cried as passengers said good-bye to relatives staying behind. We didn't have to say any sad good-byes to anyone. Our only relatives, Papa's sister and her family, were already in England. Mama had family in Germany, but I'd never met them. They wouldn't have anything to do with us because Mama married a Jew.

Crew members rushed around, loading supplies. Gulls wheeled, landed, and took off again. I heard a familiar *Kee-har* call and looked up to see a Black Headed Gull.

The Double Crossing

A man stood on the gangway with a camera, taking photos of passengers as they started up to the ship. Some of them hid their faces. All his shots seemed to be of people who looked poor. He was ignoring the nicely dressed passengers and the little children.

Another man, this one short and wearing an officer's uniform, pushed his way down the gangplank to the photographer. He acted like he was in charge and spoke angrily. He said something to the photographer, who said something back. I couldn't hear what they were saying until the officer shouted, "Get off my ship!"

The first man ignored him and started to take another picture.

"Get off—or I'll personally throw you overboard. And you can report that to the Propaganda Minister!" The officer shoved him.

That got him. The photographer stomped away, holding tight to his camera.

Papa turned to Mama. "That must be the captain. Good for him. I bet that man was taking pictures for more anti-Jewish propaganda."

I looked for the Nazi Party badge on the captain's uniform sleeves but I didn't see one. He had a little mustache, like Hitler's, but lots of men did.

• • •

When we got to the top of the gangway, a sailor in a white jacket greeted us. "Welcome aboard! May I show you to your cabins?"

He talked to us with respect, so different from the officers in the customs shed. Maybe things would be better on the ship.

"Here, let me carry those for you, ladies." The crewman reached out to take Rebekah and Mama's suitcases.

Rebekah giggled at being called a lady.

"Thank you." Mama handed over the bags.

We followed the crewman down two flights of stairs and through a hallway to our cabins in tourist class on the D deck. The thrum of the engines sounded louder the farther down we went. I was sharing a cabin with Rebekah. Our parents were next door. I looked around at twin bunks, one on each side of the room, an armchair and dresser with a mirror, and wood-paneled walls. Pretty nice.

"This one's mine!" Rebekah threw her suitcase onto one of the beds. She ran to look at the tiny bathroom. I peeked over her shoulder while she pulled back the shower curtain.

"It's perfect. Can you believe it's all ours? Come on! Let's go out. I want to see where the games are, and the swimming pool."

"This isn't a pleasure cruise," I almost said. We were running for our lives. Germany was our country. Hamburg was home. But since the Nazis smashed Papa's dentist office on *Kristallnacht*, he couldn't work. Rebekah and I were kicked out of school even though we weren't really Jewish because Mama wasn't. We were forced to leave Germany.

Still, Rebekah's excitement about the ship was contagious. We might as well try to enjoy ourselves.

"Okay." I smiled for the first time that day. "Let's explore. We have to tell Mama we're going." I grabbed my binoculars from my suitcase. They were good ones. Papa gave them to me for my birthday when I turned thirteen.

We climbed up and down staircases, wandered through hallways, peeked into the tourist class restaurant, or *saloon*, as we heard the sailors call it, and even the first-class dining saloon. Everything shone, all white tablecloths and chandeliers. A luxury ship, just like the brochure said.

We'd seen most of the ship and were looking around the upper deck. Rebekah, sounding disappointed, said, "I thought there was going to be a swimming pool here at the back. Where is it?"

A steward nearby must have heard her because he came over to us, smiling. "You heard right, young lady. We'll erect the swimming pool right here and fill it with water once we get into the warmer Gulf Stream. The name for this part of the ship, the back, is the stern, and the direction is aft. You'll soon learn the terms."

The Double Crossing

The ship wasn't supposed to leave until eight o'clock in the evening. The upper deck where we were was called the A deck. It was a perfect place to watch some of the gulls wheeling above us. I went to the rail and lifted my binoculars. There were more Black Headed Gulls, which are easy to recognize by their black heads, and some larger birds, probably Herring Gulls. I got involved in watching them and trying to identify species. Leg color. Bill color.

"Are you going to just stand here and look at birds now?" Rebekah grumbled.

I'd forgotten her. "Oh, sorry. Just give me a minute."

"That's okay. I'm going back to the cabin to get ready for dinner. Don't forget about dinner." She wagged her finger at me.

"I won't. Don't get lost." She'd be alright. She was eight, and she wouldn't get off the ship.

Rebekah rolled her eyes and skipped away.

I raised my binoculars again to look at the circling birds. When one dove into the water and came up with a small fish, others mobbed it and tried to steal the prize. Pigeons as well as gulls strutted around the quay, pecking at scraps.

A man's voice startled me. "Nice pair of Busch binoculars. I have the same model."

I turned and saw the officer with the mustache, the one who'd chased the photographer away. He was shorter than me!

"Thank you, sir. Are you the captain?"

"I am. Captain Gustav Schroeder, at your service." He held out his hand.

The HAPAG line insignia shone on his uniform. I could clearly see now that he wasn't wearing a Nazi party badge. I took the captain's hand and we shook, like two grown men.

"David Jantzen, sir."

"Welcome aboard the MS *St. Louis*, David. I see you're interested in birds."

"Yes. I love watching them. I'm learning to tell the gulls apart."

Captain Schroeder pointed to one of the large gulls down on the quay. "Do you know that one? It's a Herring Gull. And look! Here's a Caspian Tern flying over." He pointed to a large gull-like bird skimming above our heads. I aimed the binoculars at the bird with its long, bright orange bill, black cap and black legs.

"I wasn't sure about the Herring Gull, but I've seen Caspian Terns before. My father's a bird watcher too. He gave me the binoculars."

"Ah! He and I will have to have a talk. I have several books on ornithology, the science of birds. It's my hobby. Perhaps you'd like to see them sometime."

"Yes, sir. I would. Thank you."

A bell rang nearby. Another white-jacketed sailor walked toward us along the deck, swinging a hand bell.

"The steward is giving the signal for dinner," the captain said. "You'd better join your family now."

"I will. But can I ask you a question about birds?"

"If it's quick. I have to get back to the bridge."

"Will gulls follow the ship all the way across the ocean? Will we see different birds out there?"

The captain laughed. "That's two questions. Let's talk tomorrow. I tour the ship in the morning but come find me on the bridge deck after lunch. Tell Leo, my steward, I invited you." Smiling, he turned to go.

3

MS *St. Louis*
Saturday, May 13

HANNAH

WHEN I WOKE UP Saturday morning, all I could think of was my mother, sick and alone in Oldenburg, my father in the concentration camp, *Sachsenhausen*. Every time I thought about him, my stomach rolled like I might throw up. The wet, drizzly weather didn't help my mood.

After breakfast, Ruth insisted I go with her to explore the ship. I went along and tried to show some interest. Everything blurred into the background at first, with the grey and rain.

I'd never been on a ship before. After a while I started to notice things and even feel a little excited. The ship was enormous, the halls and furnishings deluxe and expensive looking. The decks had different names and letters starting with the A deck at the top. On the C deck, there were other dining saloons besides the one where we ate. We discovered a hair salon and a barber shop, and even a lady's tearoom with frilly lace tablecloths.

The Double Crossing

The best thing was a library that had shelves of books passengers could borrow. Maybe I could read my way across the ocean and stay out of the way of the Nazis. I took two adventure stories, since I was supposed to be beginning my own adventure. I chose *Emil und die Detektive* in German and *The Boxcar Children* in English. I'd studied English in school, and it wasn't hard. Many of the words were similar to German.

Ruth pointed out stacks of chairs folded away on the promenade deck. "It'll be glorious to sit out here on deck chairs in the sun. I can't wait to get out of this cold, wet weather."

We ran into a crewman who showed us what he called the "sports deck," set up to play shuffleboard or deck tennis, even a horse race game with wooden horses running around a track. No one was playing yet. Most of the passengers were still boarding.

"We're going to have such a good time." Ruth squeezed my arm.

We went down another set of stairs. When I heard men's voices nearby, singing *Heil Hitler dir*, one of the hateful Nazi party songs against Jews, my breath caught. My heart raced. For a little while, I'd almost forgotten we were on a Nazi ship.

Right after the words, "Give foreign Jews no place in your *Reich*," the singing halted. We heard a slam and jangling piano keys. The sounds were coming from a door a little way off. We tiptoed over and peeked in through a round window.

"Just what are you objecting to, Captain?" said a heavy-set man in a steward's uniform.

The small man he was talking to wore a uniform with brass buttons on the dark jacket, braid around the sleeves, and an officer's hat. He must have been the captain because he said, "I won't have you acting against my orders, Otto Schiendick, or embarrassing my passengers."

"As *Leiter* of the *Nationalsozialisten* party on board, it's my job to keep up crew morale." The pudgy steward said, taking a paper from his pocket and handing it to the captain. "This says we're authorized to use the public rooms, as long as it doesn't interfere with passengers." He spoke as if he was in charge.

The captain didn't back down. "I don't care what your paper says, or if you're the Party leader. This is my ship. You will not insult or embarrass my passengers." He thrust the paper back into the crewman's hand. "Get out! All of you! If I find you in here again, you will need more than a piece of paper to save your skins!"

Ruth tugged at my sleeve. "Let's go."

I hurried to follow her away from the door. Neither of us wanted to run into the Nazis, or the angry captain.

"The captain told that Nazi off, didn't he?" Ruth said, once we'd turned a corner.

I couldn't answer. The Nazi song had brought back the hateful things that happened to me and my family. How I'd been singled out and mocked in school. How I'd seen Father knocked to the ground when Nazis took him away in Oldenberg. The synagogue burned and in ruins. My face was hot. I wanted to yell at that Nazi *Leiter* myself.

Now I knew for sure that at least some of the crew hated us. The Nazi flag flew at the back of the ship, and we'd seen a large portrait of Hitler hanging above the stage in the social hall. Nazis were in control here too.

"Do you think they hate Jews in Cuba?" I asked Ruth.

"I don't know about Cuba. I haven't met my mother's cousin, the one we're going to stay with. But if they're letting us live in their country, they must not hate us." Ruth's smile wasn't convincing.

Any excitement I'd started to feel evaporated. I didn't want this adventure. I told Ruth I was going back to the cabin to read *The Boxcar Children*. I couldn't bear to run into any more angry, hateful people, or see another picture of Hitler glaring at me.

I tried to read, but I wasn't able to lose myself in the story. My mind kept wandering back home to my parents. It didn't help that the book was about children whose parents had died. My heart squeezed with fear.

The Double Crossing

Ruth didn't seem worried. She flitted in and out of the cabin. Each time she came back, she talked about people boarding the ship, how they were dressed, what they brought, and especially about other teenagers she'd met. She'd already made a couple of friends.

"And I talked with that cute sailor. I think he likes me."

4

MS *St. Louis*
Saturday, May 13

DAVID

I COULDN'T IMAGINE DINNER in first class being any better than what we ate in the tourist class saloon. The four of us sat at a table covered with a long, white cloth laid with china plates, crystal glasses, and silver. Musicians played at one end of the room. Waiters in white jackets took our orders from the menu. First, the appetizers. They had my favorite cheese-filled German puff pastries!

While we ate appetizers, I told Papa what had happened. "Guess what! I met the captain. You were right. He's that officer who chased the photographer away. His hobby is birds. I told him you know about birds too. He said you should talk some time."

"Hmm." Papa's fork was halfway to his mouth. He lowered it. "Well, I suppose there's no harm in that. His crew seems genuinely polite and considerate."

The rest of the menu gave us a choice of two soups, fish or rib roast, asparagus or stuffed tomatoes, French fries or potato croquettes, cookies and other desserts. I ordered *Birnenkompott*, pears in syrup, for dessert. I was so stuffed I almost couldn't finish. I don't think that had ever happened to me before. I didn't even have room for cheese, fresh fruit, and coffee afterwards. We hadn't eaten so well in years.

"It's all very grand," Mama said.

"Yes," Papa smiled. "They don't seem to have skimped on anything. Quite as if they consider us the same as any other paying passengers."

We were finishing dinner when the ship's horn blasted. I looked at the clock. It was half past seven.

Papa looked up. "They must be getting ready for the eight o'clock departure. Like I always say, we Germans are nothing if not punctual."

My legs twitched to jump up. I didn't want to miss seeing the lines cast off, and the ship pulling away from the dock into the river Elbe. But I remembered my manners. "Papa, may I be excused to go on the deck and watch?"

5

MS *St. Louis*,
Saturday, May 13 – Sunday, May 14

HANNAH

After dinner, Ruth and I went up to watch the ship depart. Most of the passengers stood at the rail, in spite of the cold and continuing drizzle. A blast from the ship's horn startled me. Under an awning on the quay, a band played one of Brahms Hungarian Dances, loud enough so we could hear it on the deck, even over the noisy activity around the ship.

A shudder under our feet and the increased roar of the engines meant the ship was about to depart. This was it! We were really leaving. There was no going back for me. I fought another wave of missing Mother and Father.

Men scurried around everywhere. They shouted commands and signaled with whistles between ship and shore. The gangway was pulled up and the men on the quay undid the ropes tying the ship. The band stopped playing and its leader saluted the *St. Louis*.

Ruth grabbed my hand. "Look! The ship's moving. We're pulling away from shore!"

The Double Crossing

People cheered. Some cried. A woman next to us stared at the shore, her face frozen. "Will we ever see our home, or our country again?"

Those words went straight to my heart. The Nazis took my home. Germany didn't want me. Mother and Father were all I had left, and I wasn't sure I'd ever see them again.

As if she knew what I was feeling, Ruth put her arm around me. We stood at the railing a long time while the *St. Louis* moved out into the murky water, past other ships, and into the middle of the Elbe. The ship rocked gently on the water as the land slid past. Finally, the sun set behind the clouds, painting them with an orange glow, and it began to get dark.

"Why the long face, Hannah, when we're starting the biggest adventure of our lives?" Ruth took my hand again. "C'mon. Let's go below. I'm getting cold."

• • •

The next morning after breakfast I went back on the deck. The ship had left the river behind and was gliding through the North Sea. I'd never been on the ocean before. I leaned on the rail of the promenade deck to watch, feeling the ship roll gently. The water looked endless. A cold, salty wind whipped my hair into tangles.

Down along the deck a boy was standing at the rail. He was tall, but he looked about my age. He wasn't wearing a uniform, so I figured he must be a passenger. But he was blond and didn't look Jewish either. Is there such a thing as an Aryan Jew? Isn't that an oxymoron? The boy held a pair of binoculars to his eyes, aiming them at a bird perched on a mast above. He was watching intently, oblivious to anything else.

Curious, I edged along the rail until I was standing pretty close, but he still didn't notice me.

"Hi. What are you looking at? That bird?"

He lowered the glasses and smiled. His eyes were warm and friendly, but blue like the eyes of those Aryan Hitler Youth boys that had terrorized the Jewish students at school. Who was he?

"I'm learning about the different kinds of gulls. That one has been holding still up there, giving me a good look."

"Oh. There are different kinds of gulls? So you're a bird watcher?"

"Yes. There are lots of different gulls, and I love learning about all the birds."

"My name's Hannah. Are you a passenger?"

"I am. I'm traveling with my family. My name's David."

"I thought all the passengers were Jewish."

"I know I don't look Jewish, and I'm not, really. My father is, but not my mother. So, as you probably know, I'm not considered Jewish—by Jews."

"But you are by Hitler and the Nazis. Even if you had only one Jewish grandparent."

"Right." David's expression turned sullen. "And by all my former friends."

Talking about Hitler made me feel gloomy and angry again.

Neither of us said anything for a minute. Then David brightened. "Hey, did you know your name, Hannah, is a palindrome?"

"That's my favorite thing about my name. It's spelled the same backwards as forwards. I know lots of other palindromes too, like *Sei fein, nie fies*, be nice, never nasty." I smiled. I was going to like him. Most people don't even know about palindromes. Another great word. Maybe making a friend and learning something about birds would be better than reading the whole trip.

6

MS *St. Louis*
Sunday, May 14

DAVID

"Will you teach me about birds?" Hannah asked. "Do you think we'll see a lot of them on the ocean?"

She wasn't shy. She started talking to me and asking questions, wanting me to teach her about birds. I liked that about her. And I liked her wild, curly red hair and green eyes, curious and sad at the same time.

"I'm just learning the sea birds, myself, mostly gulls. But almost all of them flew away after we left the harbor. If you want, though, you could come with me to visit the captain after lunch. He invited me to look at his bird books."

"You know the captain? He's not a Nazi, is he?"

"No, I don't think so. He doesn't wear the party badge. My father heard he ordered the crew to treat us respectfully and made sure the food's as good as always."

"I didn't think he was a Nazi." Hannah smiled and her eyes shone. "In that case, I'd love to meet him."

The Double Crossing

I handed Hannah the binoculars and showed her how to focus them. She caught on quickly. We talked while she looked at that last gull I'd been watching until it flew away.

When she told me her story, I understood the sadness in her eyes. Her parents weren't with her and her father was in a camp.

"You're really brave, going to Cuba without your parents. I don't know if I could do that," I said.

"Thanks. You could if you had to. I'm traveling with another girl from my town." She held her head up and didn't whine or complain like some girls would.

It was only the first day at sea and it seemed I'd already made a friend.

The weather had turned sunny. The salty smell of spray hitting the side of the ship and the wind in my face made me feel alive. I told Hannah what happened to us in Hamburg and about getting kicked out of school.

"I miss home, but it feels great not to be cooped up in our apartment anymore. They hardly let me and my sister go outside because Nazi gangs were beating people up."

After lunch, Hannah and I met on the A deck to visit the captain. I was nervous about going up to the bridge deck, but I led the way up the flight of stairs. I told the steward at the top about the captain's invitation.

"Oh, yes. He said to expect you. I'm Leo Jockl, his steward. He's in his day cabin."

Leo was young and I noticed that, like the captain, he didn't wear a Nazi badge. We followed him to the captain's cabin.

When we went in, Captain Schroeder stood up from his desk.

"Ah David. You came. Wonderful. And I see you brought a friend." He dipped his head to Hannah. "Captain Gustav Schroeder, at your service."

"Thank you. I'm Hannah Coen."

"Here are the books on ornithology I told you about, David," the captain said, taking several books from a shelf and setting them on his desk.

"You've probably already noticed the answer to the first question you asked, about gulls. They don't usually follow ships out to sea. They have their own territories. However, we do see interesting birds out on the ocean. Mainly tubenoses, of the order Procellariiformes," He turned to a page in one of his books, "petrels, shearwaters, and the like. They can drink saltwater and spend most of their lives on the open ocean. Except to breed."

"Oh. Of course. They have to drink saltwater. I never thought about that." I looked at the pictures. "I haven't seen any of these birds before. But I've heard of the albatross." I pointed to the picture of the huge, majestic bird.

"It has a wingspan of over three meters," said the captain.

"That's really big. Will we see any?" Hannah asked.

"You'll undoubtedly see some species of tubenoses, but no albatross in the North Atlantic."

We talked about different kinds of seabirds. Before we left, Captain Schroeder said, "Tell your father he's welcome to visit me. I always enjoy talking to fellow bird enthusiasts. And your parents Hannah? Are they interested in birds?"

She swallowed and straightened her shoulders. "No. And my parents are still in Germany. My father was sent to a camp."

The captain flushed. "I'm sorry. I hope they'll be able to join you soon. In Havana."

• • •

That evening, my family and I were sitting down to dinner when I saw Hannah come into the dining hall alone. She looked around as if searching for someone.

"That's my friend, Hannah. The girl I was telling you about," I said. "Can I ask her to eat with us?"

"Of course," Papa said.

Rebekah craned her head and turned around in her seat. "Oh, she's pretty!"

The Double Crossing

I waved to Hannah and got up to invite her to our table. "Are you by yourself? My family would like you to sit with us."

"Thanks. Ruth, the girl I'm traveling with, is eating with her new friends. They're all older than me."

I pulled out my chair for her and moved over so she could sit between me and Rebekah. Rebekah kept her eyes on her food, stealing shy glances at Hannah. Right away, after the introductions, Hannah started in with her questions.

"How old are you, Rebekah?"

"What do you like to do?"

"Oh! I like to read too. What are your favorite books?"

Pretty soon, my little sister lost her shyness and was talking about the story she'd just finished reading, waving her arms around and making funny voices of the characters.

"Hannah, there's going to be a movie tonight in the social hall," Mama said. "Would you like to go with us? It's supposed to be a romantic comedy."

I held my breath. I hoped she'd say yes.

She smiled. "Thank you. I would. It's awfully nice of you to invite me, Frau Jantzen."

Mama's smile lit up her blue eyes and showed her dimple. "You're welcome to join our family any time. It must be lonely for you, traveling without your parents. How old are you, dear?"

Hannah's eyes took on that sad, faraway expression again. She swallowed, like she was trying not to cry. "I'm thirteen. I do miss my mother and father terribly. But I'm not alone. I'm traveling with an older girl from my town."

Rebekah said, "You're the same age as David."

• • •

Passengers already packed the social hall when we got there for the movie, but people scooted over to let us sit together. Hannah sat between me and Rebekah again. We were crowded next to each other and I was a little embarrassed to feel Hannah's leg pressed against mine.

Hannah poked my arm. "See that steward standing in the back? The chubby one who's smirking? We saw him arguing with the captain this morning, about singing Nazi party songs. His name's something Schiendick. He's a Party *Leiter*, some kind of Nazi official."

When the lights went out and the film started, the talking stopped. But instead of the movie we were supposed to see, a newsreel began to play. It showed Hitler giving one of his horrid speeches, shouting about "worldwide Jewish influences clamoring for an interventionist war against Germany." It flashed between the speech and shots of German tanks and soldiers marching. Beside me, I felt Hannah tense. Other passengers started whispering and grumbling.

Hannah suddenly stood up. "I can't stay for this! I want to get out of here!"

"But … um." I looked around at my parents and at the other people near us. A couple of passengers behind us were already standing to leave. Then several others did. One man said, in a loud voice, "We didn't come here to see Herr Hitler or watch Nazi propaganda. I'm going to complain to the captain."

I'd been looking forward to the movie, and to spending time with Hannah. But she was right. My parents nodded and we all stood up to go. Rebekah whined a little, but Mama stooped down and whispered something to her.

As we made our way to the back of the hall, I noticed the steward, Schiendick, whispering to another crewman standing next to him. They both laughed.

Once we were on the deck, Hannah turned to me, her eyes clouded but her chin held high. "Good night, David. I'm going to my cabin." After she said good night to the rest of my family, she headed for the stairs.

Hannah's reaction to the newsreel was so different from mine. I guess I'd gotten used to the constant anti-Jewish propaganda and almost learned to ignore it. Maybe because, deep down, I didn't think it applied to me. I hadn't been brought up Jewish. Hannah took it personally. And when I thought about it, I knew she was right. I was ashamed that I didn't take it seriously enough. It *was* personal. Look where the Nazi's propaganda had gotten all of us.

7

MS *St. Louis*
Monday, May 15

Hannah

THE NEWSREEL PLAYED over and over in my mind. Was that Nazi steward, Schiendick, responsible for the insult? He'd been laughing with his friend in the back of the room. It took me a long time to fall asleep.

An announcement at breakfast told us we'd be stopping at Cherbourg, France to take on supplies, especially fresh fruits and vegetables, and more passengers. By nine-thirty, I was out on the deck with Ruth and most of the other passengers, watching as the *St. Louis* entered the harbor.

The ship anchored a little way from some docks. Smaller boats started going back and forth between a dock and the ship. Crewmen hurriedly loaded crates from the boats. I wondered why the *St. Louis* didn't anchor at the dock, and why the crewmen seemed to be rushing.

"You know what I don't see out there?" Ruth whispered. "Nazi flags."

The Double Crossing

She was right. This was France, not Germany. The only Nazis were Schiendick and the others on the ship. I said, "Thank goodness! I hope soon those swastika flags won't be seen in Germany either. Or anywhere."

When we heard that mail had been delivered, the last before Havana, we rushed to find out if there was anything for us. A long line already stretched from the Purser's office. I fidgeted. Would there be a letter from my mother? This would be the last chance until Cuba.

Finally, we reached the front of the line. There was a letter for me! I was so excited, I practically snatched it from the purser's hand. Ruth had a letter from her mother too.

We carried those letters, like precious treasures, to our cabin to read. Once I opened mine, I was disappointed to see that it barely covered one page. It had only been three days, but I was already starving for news from home.

Mother's letter began:

Liebe Hannah,

The train ride home was fine. I'm hardly coughing now. You mustn't worry about me.

She went on with some details about the train ride and plans to have dinner with Ruth's parents.

I will send letters to you in Cuba, and I'll write at once to tell you when I hear from your father. Have a wonderful sea voyage.

Not only was the letter short, it seemed too cheerful. "Mustn't worry" just made me uneasy. I did worry. Mother was still coughing, even if she said not as much. And she still hadn't heard from Father. Shouldn't he have come back before now? Of course, she must have written the letter the same day we left for it to get here already.

Quickly I scribbled a reply, so it could be posted from Cherbourg. I didn't tell her not to worry, but I tried to keep my letter cheerful too, so she would see everything was going well.

The ocean is exciting, and changes color all the time. I've made friends with a boy from Hamburg named David Jantzen, and his family. He's teaching me to use binoculars and identify birds.

I put in more details about David's family, the ship, with its dining saloons, social hall, and library, and recounted the selections on the dinner menu.

I even met the captain. He's a nice man who told me and David about sea birds. And I learned some new words: ornithology and tubenose.

I wanted to say the captain wasn't a Nazi, but I was afraid it could make trouble in case they read letters in the post. And I didn't tell her about the awful Nazis on the ship. I rushed to finish in time to mail it. At the end I just said:

I miss you, Mutter. Please take care of yourself and come soon.

I dashed to the ship's store for a stamp and mailed it.
After lunch I went back on the deck by myself. A boat brought several more passengers, including children, who boarded the ship. Some of the children ran to join parents already on board. Seeing the families hugging and hearing them say how they'd missed each other brought tears to my eyes. How I wished my mother and father were arriving and rushing to throw their arms around me. But of course, they wouldn't be. And there'd be no more stops until Cuba. No chance of anyone else joining us.

The Double Crossing

"Hi!" David came to stand next to me at the rail.

"Hi David. Wasn't that awful last night? I hope you and your family didn't mind leaving."

"No. You were right, and my parents agreed. I'm sorry I even hesitated."

"Does it seem to you like the crew are rushing?" I asked. "Are we behind schedule?"

"Papa heard a rumor that we need to get to Cuba before some other ships, or there could be a problem landing."

"But … I thought everything was settled, with the landing permits and all." My mouth went dry. Mother had said all the papers were in order.

"I thought so too. But don't worry. I'm sure it's nothing. Papa also said there are now 937 passengers on board. We're practically a village!"

I tried to smile, but I couldn't stop thinking about "a problem landing."

• • •

Early in the afternoon, the horn sounded. The *St. Louis* began to move out of the harbor toward the open Atlantic. We took turns with David's binoculars. I tried to stop thinking about problems. Instead, I focused on the big grey and white gulls David pointed out, floating on the water like little boats. Groups of them took flight to steal fish or crabs from other birds, filling the air with their hoarse cries.

David pointed out different species of birds and told me their names. Terns and pelicans flew high over the water, heads down, suddenly diving with hardly a splash. Sometimes one came up with a fish wriggling in its beak, often to be set upon by hungry gulls. Black cormorants paddled along sedately, then ducked sinuously to swim under the dark surface. Sometimes one came up with a fish in its hooked beak. I admired their grace and envied their freedom to maneuver through the air and water.

The *St. Louis* made its slow way out of the harbor and picked up speed. Its two funnels streamed identical trails of grey smoke onto the wind. Soon the birds were left behind. I stayed at the back of the ship, the stern, for some time with David. In silence we watched the white wake churn behind the ship and the coast of France disappear into the distance. Europe, and the world we knew, was lost behind us. Cuba was totally unknown. What would it be like? How soon would Mother and Father come?

• • •

After dinner I took a walk around the decks. Sunset colored the 360 degree horizon. There was no longer any sign of land. Near the foredeck, I spotted a couple of younger girls crouched over something. One of them was David's sister, Rebekah. Whatever they were looking at was making a noise, a *pee-pee-pee*. I went closer and leaned over the girls' shoulders. It was a little black bird, not much bigger than a sparrow, with long wings. It kept trying to get up from the deck. Its feet were webbed like a duck's. Instead of standing on them, it squatted on the lower part of its legs, flapping one wing, and trying to lift onto its toes. The other wing dragged.

"Rebekah," I said. "What happened?"

"We found it like this. Maybe it flew into a window." She looked ready to cry. Her dark eyes were serious, like her father's. "What should we do?"

"Go get David. I passed him a while ago, on the aft deck with his binoculars. He'll know."

They ran off, leaving me to stand watch over the little bird. The poor thing must have been scared to death. It was hurt and probably felt cornered. I was afraid of hurting it more if I tried to pick it up. And I didn't know how fierce it might be. Its bill wasn't very big, but it looked pointed and sharp. In a few minutes, Rebekah and her friend came back with David.

"Oh, it's a sea bird. I think it's a petrel, one of those tubenoses Captain Schroeder showed us in his book. Let's take it to him."

"But if we pick it up, won't it flap and hurt itself?" I asked. "Or peck us?"

"I know a trick. If you cover birds, they get quiet and even fall asleep. At least some birds do." He took off his sweater and carefully dropped it over the fluttering bird.

"It worked!" said Rebekah's friend. "It stopped flapping."

David wrapped the sweater around the bird and picked it up. It didn't make a sound. "It weighs almost nothing. Rebekah, just me and Hannah should go."

"No fair! We found it first."

"I know. But it would be too many people in the captain's cabin. He already knows us. He talked to us about birds."

The girls plodded off, grumbling.

I felt sorry for the little girls. They did find the bird first. But I followed David to the bridge deck to find the captain.

• • •

Captain Schroeder put aside some papers spread on his worktable to make room for the bird. He gently unwound David's sweater.

"You're right. It's a petrel. A European Storm Petrel, to be precise. They spend all their time at sea, except during breeding. Cover his head, David, and hold him while I take a look."

The captain stretched out the bird's wing showing a white patch on its rump and another under the wing. It smelled fishy. I noticed its feet had only three toes, with a web between.

"Is something wrong with its legs?" I said. "It just squats on them. Why doesn't it walk?"

"These birds don't spend much time on land. When they do, they don't walk, but tiptoe, flapping their wings. It doesn't look like the wing's broken, only sprained. I expect it will be able to fly again in a few days. It's a young bird, probably come north a bit early."

"What's that lump on its beak?" I pointed at a bulge near the top of the upper bill. "Is that supposed to be there?"

"It's the gland that filters out salt so the bird can drink seawater. That's why they're called tubenoses." Captain Schroeder lightly touched the lump.

"It has a funny smell," I said. "Like an animal."

"That's right. Petrels generally have a musky odor, kind of like a weasel," the captain said.

"Can we keep it?" David and I said at the same time. We looked at each other and smiled.

"I mean," he said, "just to take care of it until it can fly?"

"Oh yes! Please let us help it," I said.

"Hmm," the captain stroked the bird's glossy, black feathers. "There's a superstition about storm petrels. Many sailors believe they bring bad luck, or bad weather. I wouldn't want word to get around among the crew that it's on board."

"I could keep it in my cabin." David looked hopeful.

Captain Schroeder shook his head. "That won't work. A steward goes in to clean every day."

A quick knock came on the door and Leo Jockl, the captain's steward, opened it. "Oh, excuse me. I didn't know you had company." He hesitated. He looked so young. I guessed he was only a few years older than us.

"Come in, Leo. What is it?"

"The radio officer asked me to tell you there's another transmission from the HAPAG office."

Captain Schroeder frowned. "Sorry, children. I must go to the radio room. Leo, please help them find a place to keep this bird safe but hidden." He handed the bird back to David. "Find a box for them to put it in. And they'll need something to feed it. Fish scraps from the kitchen, maybe."

He started out the door, then turned back to Leo. "It's better I don't know where it is. You know how some of the crew feel about storm petrels."

As he left the cabin, he muttered, "Why doesn't HAPAG tell me if there's a problem? What's happening in Havana, anyway?"

The Double Crossing

A flutter of fear tightened my stomach. It seemed even the captain was worried about problems in Cuba.

8

MS *St. Louis*
Monday, May 15 – Tuesday, May 16

DAVID

A PROBLEM? Captain Schroeder disappeared before I could ask. Hannah shot me a worried look.

"Let's see the bird." Leo didn't seem to notice our worry. "Oh, it's a pretty little thing. Storm petrel, eh? I've seen flocks of them, fluttering like bats or running across the water, but never this close."

I looked back at the bird. "They run on water?"

"Yes. Flapping their wings and dipping their beaks in to scoop up something to eat."

I liked Leo. He noticed birds, and his friendly brown eyes reminded me of Rebekah's. He asked us to wait while he went to find a box.

"I think he needs a name." Hannah stroked the bird in my hands. "How about Peter, for petrel?"

"Perfect."

"What do you think the captain meant about a problem?" she asked.

The Double Crossing

"I don't know. Probably nothing." I didn't want to think about it. We wouldn't get to Cuba for days and by then it would all be figured out. "Maybe it has to do with those other ships that we're supposed to stay ahead of."

Soon Leo came back with a small wooden crate. "I have an idea about where to keep it. We can put it in one of the lifeboats, under the cover. Even if it makes some noise, I don't think anyone will notice out there. You can climb in to take care of it without being seen if you're careful."

I wrapped Peter in my sweater again, and Leo brought along the crate. Outside, it was starting to get dark. We walked back along the port side of the ship. A few passengers went by on their way to a dance. The women's hair was crimped and they wore high heels. The men were dressed up too, in suits and ties.

"Good evening," they said as they passed us.

Leo stopped at one of the farthest aft pairs of lifeboats. They hung from what Leo called "davits," one of the pair slightly above the deck, the other higher with a gap of about a meter between them. No one was around. Leo put down the crate. He worked on the ropes that held down the lifeboat cover, unhooked an edge on the back side, and lifted it. While he did that, I gently set the little bird into the crate. He stayed very still.

Before I closed the lid, Hannah reached in and stroked his feathers.

Leo held open the lifeboat cover. "Go ahead and climb inside. Use the rail to boost yourself up. I'll pass the crate to you. Set it on the floor between the thwarts."

"Thwarts?" I asked.

"The benches that go across."

The lifeboat was tied down so well it didn't sway at all when I climbed in. It was almost dark now, and even darker inside. I ducked beneath the upper boat and stepped into the well between two of the benches, where I could squat and fit under the cover. After I found a place for the crate, I stuck my head out.

"What about food and water?"

"I'll get some fish scraps and something to put water in," Leo said.

"I think he might need saltwater. But I'm not sure."

"I'll bring fresh and saltwater. Be right back."

Hannah climbed into the lifeboat and squatted near me. I could barely see her. The lifeboat was big, but the space was broken up by the benches, as well as oars stowed along each side, and crates of what were probably emergency supplies. I noticed a faint smell of fresh paint. We were cramped, hunkered under the cover.

"I hope we'll be able to take care of him okay," Hannah said. "Do you really think he'll be able to fly again?"

"Captain Schroeder seems to know what he's talking about. He knows a lot about birds."

Leo came back with bowls of water and fish scraps. We set them in the crate with Peter, closed the lid, and climbed out. After we pulled the lifeboat cover closed, Leo hooked it so it looked like it was fastened but would be easier to raise next time.

"Thank you, Leo," we both said.

"This is fun. Make sure no one's around when you look in on the bird. I'll meet you here tomorrow, right after breakfast, and see what you need." He smiled and left.

"What a nice boy," Hannah said. "I hope Peter will be all right. Do you think it's okay to leave him?"

"He'll be okay for the night. Let's meet here in the morning before breakfast."

When I got back to our cabin, Rebekah pestered me until I told her what we'd done with the bird.

"But don't go there. If anyone sees you poking into the lifeboat, there could be trouble." I told her about the sailors' superstition.

"That's silly." She argued, but finally promised to stay away. "But you have to promise when you let it go, you'll let me and Liesl come too. Remember, we found it."

"Fair enough, Bekah," I said.

The Double Crossing

• • •

The next morning, Hannah was at the lifeboat when I got there, peeking under the cover. No one else was around. We climbed in and pulled the cover back down. The smell of the bird, what Captain Schroeder called musky, was stronger in the covered space. No sounds came from inside the box. When we took off the lid, we found the little petrel sitting in that funny way, like squatting on his haunches. He stared at us, breathing fast, making that *pee-pee-pee* sound. Probably a warning or distress call.

Hannah stroked Peter with one finger. "I don't think he's eaten any of the fish. Don't birds need to eat pretty often?"

"I think so. We should ask the captain or ask Leo to ask him. I think I'll tell Papa too. He'll keep it secret. He knows a lot about birds."

• • •

At breakfast, I didn't think other people could hear me, there was so much noise with people talking, waiters taking orders, and silverware clinking. I told Papa about the bird.

"How often do you think it should eat?"

Rebekah, of course, was listening, hanging on every word. Mama seemed interested too.

"Why is this such a secret?" she asked.

I told them what the captain said about sailors' superstitions. Mama laughed and Papa shook his head.

"I don't know about the eating habits of these birds," Papa said. "Captain Schroeder probably knows more about sea birds."

After breakfast, Hannah went with me back to the lifeboat. More people were strolling on the deck, so Hannah stayed on lookout while I climbed in to check on Peter. He seemed okay, but still hadn't eaten. The fish scraps were beginning to smell. I couldn't tell if he'd drunk any water. I got out and we waited for Leo, who arrived a couple of minutes later.

"How's our little friend?"

In a rush, talking over each other, we told him we were worried that the bird wasn't eating.

"Can we ask the captain, or can you?"

"What should we do?"

"How long can he go without eating?"

Leo frowned. "I'll go ask Captain Schroeder right now. You wait here."

It took a while, but finally Leo came back. "The captain checked his books and learned that storm petrels won't eat in captivity. He said we have to try to feed him, to push fish down his throat." He showed us a little paper wrapped package. "I brought some fresh fish scraps."

Making sure the coast was clear, all three of us climbed into the lifeboat. It was awkward and crowded, but we squeezed in. Leo whispered, "I'll hold him while you feed him. Captain says don't feed him too much at one time."

Hannah looked a little pale. "He's so small. I'm afraid we'll hurt him."

"Me too. But he has to eat. I'll hold his beak open and you put the fish in. You have the smallest fingers," I said.

Carefully, I pried open Peter's narrow beak. The top bill had that funny tubenose bump near the base and curved down at the tip. It was surprising how wide the beak opened. Hannah took a tiny piece of fish and dropped it inside the open mouth, but the bird's tongue pushed it away.

"Captain said you have to push it into his throat," Leo said. "Then try massaging his neck to make him swallow."

"Push it?" Hannah's hand trembled, but she reached in with one slim finger and pushed the piece of fish down into the bird's throat. I closed the beak while she stroked Peter's neck until he swallowed.

Hannah shuddered. "It seems awful to force him like this. Do you think it hurts?"

I wondered that too.

The Double Crossing

"The captain told me it wouldn't harm the bird if we're gentle. It's kind of like a mother bird feeding a baby, isn't it?"

Hannah made a face. "I don't feel like a mother bird."

"You won't hurt him, Hannah," Leo said. "You're being very gentle."

We went on feeding Peter, tiny bit by tiny bit. It took a long time. Every little while Leo would peek out under the cover to make sure no one was around. Gradually we relaxed and talked in low whispers, getting to know each other.

Then Leo whispered, "What was it like, being Jewish in Germany?"

I froze. I hadn't even told my family much about the horrible day I was forced to leave school. Hannah and I looked at each other. I couldn't say anything.

"Kind of like what's happening to Peter," she said. "He's trapped and can't get out. He probably feels scared and helpless."

As we finished the slow process of feeding Peter, the frown stayed on Hannah's face, like she was still thinking about Leo's question. I was too. My heart pounded. I wanted to be friends with Leo, but I didn't know how to talk about what happened.

When it seemed like Peter had eaten enough, Hannah stroked his head. She began to talk about how her teacher made an example of her and the other Jewish girls.

"Our new Nazi teacher treated us Jewish girls like we weren't even people! She made us stand in front of the class and said, 'I want you all to notice the differences that mark these girls as Jews, not Aryans like true Germans. Look at the shape of Eva Aaron's nose, Hannah Coen's frizzy red hair, and Judith Weiss's forehead.' It was horrible! She poked us and pointed." Hannah's lips curled a little, almost in a snarl. Tears sparkled in her eyes. "I refused to go back after that day."

"The pig!" Hannah's story made me feel hot and angry. "Something like that happened to me. I was called to the Director's office at school, with all the Jewish boys. 'You boys collect your things and go home,' the director told us. 'The government has decreed you aren't allowed to attend school with German students.' He said that Jews weren't German under the new laws."

My face was burning. "I told him I wasn't Jewish because my family isn't religious, and my mother isn't Jewish. That only made him mad."

What I still couldn't say was what the Director had called me. "David Jantzen, you are the product of a union between German and Jew. You are an abomination!"

Leo frowned and shook his head. "I'm sorry. Those things should never have happened to either of you, to anyone."

"After that, my parents wouldn't allow me and my sister to go out." I looked down at Peter. "So I know what it's like to be trapped in a box."

• • •

When we met again in the evening to feed Peter, Leo rushed up, flushed and upset. "*Der Saukerl*, Schiendick, took me aside today and asked me to spy on Captain Schroeder. Schiendick's a big Nazi. He doesn't like the captain because he's not in the Party, and he doesn't support all that Nazi stuff."

"Schiendick's a supercilious nincompoop," Hannah said.

Hannah sure likes her fancy words, I thought.

Leo shook his head. "Can you believe it? He wanted me to listen in and report to him on the captain's activities. When I told him 'no,' he said he was putting me on 'his list.' He said, 'watch your step, Jokl.'

"He's got it in for me now."

9

MS *St. Louis*
Wednesday, May 17

HANNAH

I JERKED AWAKE when the ship gave a lurch. It rolled from side to side. I grabbed onto my bed rail and climbed out of the bunk, barely keeping my balance. It was light outside and mountains of water rose higher than the porthole before crashing as waves against the ship and covering the glass. I heard Ruth in the little bathroom, throwing up.

"Are you all right?" I called through the closed door. "Do you need anything?"

After a minute, Ruth opened the door. She was nearly as pale as the porcelain sink behind her. "Maybe some tea? And a cracker?"

I made my way to the dining saloon on the C deck, one level up, staggering and grasping the handrail. Now I understood why there were rails everywhere on the ship. Fortunately, the rolling motion didn't bother my stomach.

Few people had made it to the dining saloon for breakfast. David and his sister sat alone at their table. I joined them.

"Ruth is seasick. A lot of other people must be too."

"Papa is sick, and Mama a little," said Rebekah. "She stayed to take care of him."

"I'm going to bring Ruth some tea and toast. You could take some to your parents too."

We ordered the tea and toast to take to our cabins and ate our breakfasts quickly. As we stood to go, David whispered, "Leo's going to meet us at the boat. Come as soon as you can."

I nodded.

• • •

When I got back to the cabin, Ruth was in bed, looking a little less pale. I put the tea and toast on her bedside table. She sat up and took a sip of tea.

"Anything else you need?" I asked.

"Not now," she said. "Thanks. I'm supposed to be the one looking after you on this trip."

I hurried to the lifeboat. David and Leo were already there. David and I climbed in under the cover. As soon as we removed the lid of Peter's box, the little petrel raised his wings, flapped them a couple of times, and lifted onto his toes.

"Look!" I said. "He's standing up. He's moving both wings. I think he's better already."

David picked Peter up and felt each wing before putting him back in the crate. "He does seem better." He poked his head out to talk to Leo, who was still standing on the deck. "Would you ask Captain Schroeder what we should do?"

"Yes. I'll let you know what he says this evening. In the meantime, here's the fish I brought." He handed a packet to David. "I need to get back to my duties. We have a lot of miserable passengers."

"Thanks, Leo," David said. "See you after dinner?"

"Right." He looked up and down the boat deck before walking away.

Soon after David put the cover back down, we heard footsteps approach. Whoever it was stopped close by. I heard the scratch of a match and smelled cigarette smoke.

There was enough light, even under the lifeboat cover, for me to see David's eyes widen. He put a finger to his lips and held the bird close. Cigarette smoke drifted under the cover.

"There goes Jockl," a man's voice said with contempt. "I wonder what he's up to. He's a Jew lover like the captain. He'd better watch out. I've got my eye on him."

Another man's voice said, "I wouldn't want to be on your bad side, Otto."

I tensed in every muscle. The first man must be Otto Schiendick! David and I looked at each other.

"Hey!" continued the second man, "Don't you think it's funny how these Jews are puking their guts out?" They both laughed. "A little rough sea, and they can't take it. Why are we going so fast on this new course anyway? What's the big hurry?"

"I don't know, but I'll find out." That was Schiendick again. "The sooner we get to Havana, the better for me. I've got an important mission there."

"A mission? For the Party?"

"Not just the Party. Listen Heinrich, can I trust you to keep a secret? I may need your help. And I'm going to have to hide something in our cabin."

"Don't worry. You can trust me. I won't say a word to anyone."

"You know I'm doing important work. You're here because I got them to assign you and the other Gestapo as firemen. I needed loyal Party men to help keep an eye on this boatload of Jews." The word was followed by the sound of spitting.

"I know. I've heard you're really coming up in the Party."

Schiendick lowered his voice almost to a whisper and said, "That work for the Gestapo is not my only mission. I have a job for the *Abwehr*. I'm meeting a connection in Havana who's going to give me documents to take back to Germany."

The Double Crossing

"The *Abwehr*? Military intelligence? *Mein Gott!* I didn't know," said the other man, Heinrich. "Of course I'll help. Whatever you need."

David and I held absolutely still, leaning forward to hear.

"Good. It's essential I get this information and take it to Germany. But rumor is we could have a problem landing in Havana." Someone exhaled smoke. "Remember, this is top secret. I don't know all the details, but it's classified information about the U.S. military. And in case I need your help, you should know that the code name is Operation Sunshine."

"*Unglaublich!* Incredible!" Heinrich sounded impressed. "You can count on me, Otto."

"I knew I could. You're a loyal Party member."

Their footsteps moved away. I peeked under the edge of the canvas cover to look after them. Schiendick's wide shape was unmistakable. Heinrich was taller, thinner, and had a thatch of black hair. I watched until they were out of sight.

"David, what are we going to do? They're Gestapo! Schiendick is a spy."

David frowned "Schiendick's a rat and a spy, but once we're in Cuba, what will it matter? I mean, as long as the Gestapo are just 'keeping an eye,' on us. I'm sure Captain Schroeder won't let them do anything against his passengers."

"But what about the military secrets? Who should we tell?" Why wasn't David more upset? Couldn't he see we had to do something? The Nazis were evil.

"I don't know that we have to tell anyone. They aren't going to do anything until Havana. Come on. We can talk quietly while we feed Peter." He held the bird against his chest and pried its beak open.

I began to push little pieces of fish into Peter's throat. Doesn't David understand how important this is? But he's right about one thing. Nothing will happen until Havana. We have time to think about it. Make a plan.

"I wonder what they meant about a new course, and being in a hurry," I whispered. "And why do we keep hearing about a problem landing in Havana?"

"Maybe Leo knows. We'll ask him this evening."

As I pushed one tiny piece of fish after another into Peter's throat, I thought about the disturbing things we'd heard earlier.

"I don't like how everything's adding up. First they were in a hurry to leave Cherbourg. Then you heard something about getting to Havana ahead of some other ships. And when we were in the captain's cabin and Leo came in? Captain Schroeder was upset about that radio transmission from HAPAG headquarters, about a problem."

"Maybe you're making too big a thing of it. Little problems probably come up on any Atlantic crossing."

When we finished feeding Peter, we went to our cabins to take care of our seasick traveling companions. I spent the rest of the morning and early afternoon bringing tea to Ruth and giving her a wet cloth after she threw up. I had to breathe through my mouth to keep the smell of vomit from making me sick too.

By midafternoon the sea calmed, and the ship stopped rolling. Ruth was able to keep down the tea and toast I brought. Soon after, she felt well enough that she wanted to go on the deck for some fresh air.

"I'm fine now. It's amazing how you can go from being so sick you want to die, to feeling normal, almost as soon as the motion stops. Thanks ever so much for taking care of me. I release you from your nursing duties."

I actually laughed a little. Something I hadn't done in a while.

When we arrived on the deck, Ruth and I savored the cool breeze and took deep breaths of salty air. She gave me a little push. "Go have fun."

I wasn't thinking about fun. Schiendick's words kept running through my head. Why were Gestapo men on the ship anyway? Why firemen? The idea of the ship catching fire was terrifying. And what should we do about his spy mission?

After I left Ruth, I found David in the lifeboat with Peter. No one was around and I climbed in with him.

"Are your parents feeling better?"

"Yes. Papa had it pretty bad, but he's all right now. He and Mama are sitting out in deck chairs, taking some sun."

I peeked out to make sure no one was coming, "I don't understand why you're not upset about this spy thing. Now that we know, we have to try to stop them."

"Why?" he said.

"Think about it. Why are the Nazis stealing information about the U.S. military? Maybe Hitler plans to start a war. The Americans helped defeat Germany in the Great War. He might think they'd fight again. Or he might even plan to attack them."

His eyes widened. "I didn't think about it like that. I just thought it didn't concern us."

We heard footsteps coming close and froze. Someone lifted the lifeboat cover! What a relief when we saw Leo's face looking in.

"Oh good, you're here. Captain Schroeder wants to see the bird. He has some time now."

"Great!" David reached for the crate. He handed it to Leo and we both climbed out.

"Wait a minute, Leo," I said. "Before we go, I wanted to ask you a couple of questions."

"Go ahead," Leo said. "Let's talk as we walk."

David took the crate back from Leo and we started toward the stairs to the bridge deck.

"Why are there firemen on the ship? Are fires common?"

Leo chuckled. "Firemen on a ship are unskilled men who work in the engine room. The term is left over from steam engines, when firemen stoked the engines with coal. But this is a motor ship, that's why she's MS *St. Louis*. For motor ship. She runs on diesel."

"That's a relief. I hated thinking about the ship catching fire. And why did we speed up today? Did the ship change course? Is there a problem?"

Leo stopped and motioned us into the space between a couple of lifeboats. He lowered his voice.

"Passengers will probably know soon enough, but don't say anything yet. The captain's been getting messages from the headquarters office about the British *Orduña* and the French *Flandre*, two smaller ships that are also carrying Jewish refugees to Havana. They aren't far behind us. HAPAG wants us to get there first."

"Why?" I asked. "What difference does it make?"

Leo cleared his throat. "Well, um, we get reports on the news from home. Goebbels' propaganda ministry has been putting out a lot of stuff against Jews, and especially against the passengers on the *St. Louis*. It looks like they're trying to get the Cubans to change their minds about letting you in. At noon today, in the news summary the captain got, they called our passengers subhuman, *Untermenschen*."

"What!" My voice was too loud.

"Shh!" Leo looked around. "Don't worry. Captain Schroeder swears he'll get you all to Cuba and safely off the ship. That's why he's in a hurry. Our chances are better if we get there before those other ships."

"It doesn't make sense," David said.

"No, it doesn't," I said. "The Nazis were so anxious to get us out of Germany. Why wouldn't they want us to land in Cuba?"

"C'mon," Leo said. "Let's get the bird up to the captain while he's got time."

10

MS *St. Louis*
Wednesday, May 17

David

I FOLLOWED LEO, carrying Peter's box. Hannah was right behind me. I kept thinking about what she said. I couldn't understand either why the Nazis would want the *St. Louis'* passengers to go back to Germany. They'd wanted to be rid of us.

And there was the problem of Schiendick. Okay, he was a spy. So why should it matter to me if the Nazis were spying on the Americans? I wasn't American. Maybe Hitler was planning to start a war. But even if he did, people said the Americans wouldn't get involved in another war in Europe. What could Hannah and I do anyway? Tell the captain? Sure, the captain was nice, and he treated his Jewish passengers with respect. He wasn't a Nazi. But he was still a German officer.

I turned to look at Hannah and the frown on her face told me she must be worrying too.

• • •

The Double Crossing

"Come in," called Captain Schroeder when Leo knocked. He had one of his ornithology books open on the desk to the page on storm petrels.

The captain closed the book and moved it out of the way. "Set the box down here and let's look at our little guest."

As always, the captain was crisp and official in his uniform, though he wasn't wearing his hat.

I set the box down and opened it. Peter stretched to peer over the side. Almost at once he began flapping his wings and seemed about to take off. I reached for him and held him with his wings folded against his body.

"Looks like he's moving that wing as well as the other now." Captain Schroeder reached out for him. "Here, let me see."

I handed Peter to the captain, who stretched open the tapered wings. First one, then the other. His small hands were gentle and efficient. The bird held still, turning his head to watch out of one round black eye, as the captain felt along each wing. When he finished, he handed Peter back to me. "You two have done an excellent job caring for him. It's only been what? A couple of days? But looks like he's healed."

"What shall we do?" Hannah asked.

"He should be able to fly now. Go down to B deck. It's closest to the water. Take him to the back of the ship. When you're ready, open the box. He'll take it from there."

"Thank you for all your help," I said as I settled Peter back into the box.

"Yes, thank you, sir," said Hannah.

"Leo, you can go too, if you like," said the captain. "You've been involved with the bird's care."

As soon as the three of us were outside the captain's cabin, I said, "I have to go find my sister. Remember, we promised her and her friend they could watch when we let him go? Can you take him down?" I handed the crate to Hannah. "But don't let him go until we come!"

I hurried down the stairs, and across the deck. I practically flew down the next three levels to our cabin. When I burst in, I was glad to find Rebekah there with her friend, whose name I didn't remember.

"Hey!" Rebekah ran into the bathroom and stuck her head out. "Knock before you come barging in next time."

Clothes were piled on her bed. I hadn't noticed that she was only wearing her slip. It looked like a dress to me.

A little out of breath from the stairs, I told the girls we were about to release the storm petrel. "On the lower … aft deck. Hurry up and … get dressed. Meet us there." I grabbed my binoculars.

"You better wait for us!" Rebekah yelled as I ran out.

• • •

After everyone arrived, including Leo, who hurried up at the last minute, we were ready. I opened the box for the last time. Peter flapped his wings and stood up on his toes like he had before. A few nearby passengers came closer to see.

"Stand back, everyone. Give him room," Leo said.

Peter fluttered out of the box. He landed on the deck and ran a little way, still on his toes, flapping his wings.

"Oh my," a woman said. "What a pretty little bird!"

It was exciting to be so close when Peter jumped into the air. He spread his wings and flew almost like a bat, fluttering and swooping. The glossy black wings and white rump shone against the dark blue sea below. He called a fast *wick-wick-wick*, a very different sound from the distress call we'd heard him make before. He swooped away and down until he reached the surface of the ocean. I lifted my binoculars to watch. For a moment, he seemed to be running on the water, still fluttering his wings. Then he settled down to float. Soon he was too far behind for us to see.

Everyone cheered.

"That was amazing," Hannah said. "Did you see how he walked on the water? Just like you said, Leo."

The Double Crossing

I felt bad when I realized I hadn't shared the binoculars. It was all so fast.

"The captain told me that's why they're called petrels," said Leo. "Because they walk on water, like Saint Peter."

"You chose the right name for him, Hannah," I said.

"Wow!" said Rebekah. "He got better so fast. And now he's free! But we should go, or we'll be late for dinner. Papa and Mama will wonder where we are." She and her friend ran off.

"I've got to go too. It's time to serve the captain his dinner." Leo rushed toward the stairs to the upper decks.

Hannah and I stayed a little longer, looking out at the ocean. Sunlight still shone on the upper decks, but below, the water had turned dark. Ahead of the ship, the sun was setting. Rose-colored clouds hung behind us.

"Isn't it beautiful?" Hannah looked toward the sunset. Her face shone rosy and her red hair was a fiery halo. I couldn't help thinking she looked beautiful. Heat rose into my face. I hoped my blush was camouflaged by the sunset glow.

I wanted to talk to her, but I suddenly felt tongue-tied. I stammered, "H-Have dinner with us?"

11

MS *St. Louis*
Thursday, May 18

Hannah

David and I swam in the pool with his sister Rebekah and her friend. Later we played shuffleboard with Ruth. We didn't have Peter to take care of, but I liked spending time with him. And he was the only other person who knew about Schiendick. Surely he'd want to help me stop Operation Sunshine.

After lunch, we went to look for sea birds.

Standing at the rail together, we scanned the ocean in silence. My mind began to chew on all the upsetting things we'd heard. The propaganda attacks. The race against those other ships. I didn't notice my hands clenching the rail until David said, "Is something wrong?"

"I'm sorry." I took a breath and tried to relax. "I keep thinking about what Leo told us. What if the Cubans don't want us? Will they send us back to Germany?"

It wouldn't be so bad to go back to Mother. But they might send us to a camp, like Father. They could already have sent Mother! I bit the inside of my cheek and tasted blood.

"Don't worry. The Cubans charged a lot for those landing permits. They have to let us in." David turned back to scanning for birds.

All I could see was water and sky. I couldn't stop worrying.

"There! A couple of storm petrels." He pointed and passed me the binoculars.

The funny little birds took my mind off my fears. I laughed to see the way they pattered, almost dancing, along the ocean's surface, dipping their beaks to pick up tiny fish or something.

"Do you think one of them is Peter?" I said.

"Could be. He's out there somewhere."

A flock of grey and white birds caught my eye. I pointed. "Over there. Are those gulls? But aren't we too far from land?" The birds were flying low over the water and diving for fish. I handed the binoculars back to David.

He watched for a few minutes. "I think they're fulmars. I saw them in the captain's book. Take another look." He gave back the binoculars. "See how they hold their wings stiff? They don't flap as much as gulls. And they have those bumps on the upper part of their bills. Tubenoses."

"Oh, yeah, I can see the bump. Like Peter. For getting rid of the salt in the water. That's so amazing."

I gave the binoculars back to David. He went on watching the birds, but my mind kept whirring. Finally, I had to say it, "What are we going to do about Schiendick and his Operation Sunshine? Have you told your father? Or anyone? We've got to stop him getting those spy secrets back to the Nazis."

"No. I haven't told anyone." He lowered the binoculars. "I've been thinking about what you said and I think you're right. We should try to stop the Nazis from getting military secrets. But I don't know who we could tell. Sounds like Schiendick has a lot of influence. Even the captain might get in trouble."

"The captain's the only one who can do something. He could lock Schiendick up."

David put a finger to his lips. My voice had gotten louder and two women passengers walking by were giving us curious looks.

"We don't get to Cuba until the twenty-seventh," David said once the women were out of hearing. "Let's keep an eye on Schiendick, try to learn more about his plan."

"I know he can't do anything until we get there. But once we do, it might be too late. We'll be getting off the ship. There'll be lots of excitement. That's when someone's got to watch Schiendick. And stop him."

"Calm down," David said. "We might find out there's something we can do before then. Once we know more."

"All right. But if we don't have a plan to stop him before we get to Havana, we'll tell someone, like the captain, or Leo, or your father. Promise?"

David nodded. "I promise."

As we headed back to our cabins to get ready for dinner, he asked, "Are you going to the movie tonight?"

My heart gave a little jump. Why was he asking?

"Um, I don't know," I said. "What movie is it?"

"It's Robin Hood, with Errol Flynn. I didn't get to see it in Germany, because, you know … they didn't let Jews into movie theaters." He was so distracted he almost ran into a little girl jumping rope. "Oh, sorry," he said, stepping around her.

"I really wanted to see it. It made me so mad." We walked a little farther, then David stopped. "So I was wondering …" He looked at his feet, then at the ocean. Anywhere, it seemed, but at me. "Uh … Want to go? With me, I mean?"

Heat rose in my face. Was this like a date? Or just friends? Butterflies danced in my stomach. "Okay. Sure. That would be fun. As long as they don't show more Hitler propaganda."

12

MS *St. Louis*
Friday, May 19

DAVID

Last night during some of the exciting parts of the movie, Hannah reached over and took my hand. Holding her hand, I felt excited and nervous, and my hand got all sweaty, which was embarrassing.

I was thinking about that on the way to breakfast when Rebekah asked, "Why are you smiling?"

"Oh, nothing. I mean, I was thinking about the movie last night."

She gave me a curious look. "You're blushing."

As soon as we arrived in the dining saloon, I looked around for Hannah. She wasn't there.

After we gave the steward our order, Papa said, "Your friend Hannah's a nice girl. Seems like you really like her, David. Did she go to the movie with you last night?"

Before I could answer, Rebekah sang, "David's got a girlfriend."

"Rebekah," Mama said, "Don't be rude. Papa wasn't talking to you."

"Um. She is nice. And … uh … she did go with me to the movie. I like her." I gave Rebekah a serious look. "But she's not my girlfriend. So don't say that."

As we were getting up from the table, Hannah came in with Ruth. I waved to her and she waved back, then came over to say hi.

"Want to do something later?" she said.

"Sure," I said, my heart speeding up again. "Meet you on the A deck."

When I went back down to get my binoculars, I was surprised to find a man leaving my cabin, and alarmed when I recognized the chubby steward. It was Otto Schiendick! Was he on to us? I stopped dead in front of him.

"Hey! What were you doing in there?"

"Oh, excuse me, Jew boy." Schiendick smirked and pushed past me. He "accidentally" bumped me with a bucket of cleaning supplies he was carrying. "I'm your steward. That means I have the unpleasant duty of cleaning up after you every day."

I tensed at the insult. But, hateful as the Nazi Schiendick was, this could be my chance to find out more. I swallowed my anger.

"I'm sorry. You surprised me. Do you, um, clean the same cabins every day? How many?"

"Yes. Every day I'm responsible for the same twenty-five tourist cabins on D deck. So, as you can see, this is no pleasure cruise for me."

"Oh, sure. But, do you do anything else?" Schiendick probably wasn't going to tell me he spied for the *Abwehr*, or even that he was the Nazi Party *Leiter*. But any information might help.

"I don't have time to chat with you, even if I wanted to. I have a lot of work to do." Schiendick turned his back and went down the hall to the next room, my parents' room, opened the door with a key, and disappeared inside.

What a nasty man! Even if I hadn't known he was a Nazi and a spy, I would have despised him. I inspected my room. I had to admit the bunks were neatly made, and everything was clean. My binoculars were sitting where I'd left them. Nothing seemed to be missing. I probably couldn't add "thief" to Schiendick's list of crimes. I grabbed the binoculars and went up on the deck.

When I found Hannah, I told her about seeing Schiendick.

"Hmm. That's good. Now we know where he works. We need to catch him talking to his friend again, or …" A spark shone in her green eyes. "If we could search his cabin."

Search his cabin? What was she thinking? Hannah was taking this spy thing too far.

"We can't. The crew quarters are off limits to passengers."

"Well, at least we can hang around and see when he takes his breaks." She tapped her fingers on the rail. "He probably goes on deck for a smoke. If he meets up with his friend then, we might be able to learn something. Like who's his contact in Havana and how he's going to get the information." She smiled, as if she'd already solved the puzzle.

"All right. Tomorrow I'll check back at my room a bunch of times, try to see when he takes a break. But let's forget about it for now and go for a swim."

Hannah shook her head at me, but said, "Okay. For now."

We passed the rest of that day like carefree tourists on a cruise across the Atlantic. I'd been self-conscious in my bathing suit the first time we swam, but Hannah hadn't seemed shy, and now I wasn't either. She gathered most of her wild hair back into a ponytail and swam gracefully. Afterwards, we tried our hands at deck tennis and even the horse race game, though it was more for younger kids.

• • •

The dinner menu listed eggs with caviar, boiled turbot in sauce romaine, German style ribs, several soups, salads and desserts. I'd never tasted caviar before and found it a little salty and a little fishy. When I bit into them, the tiny eggs popped in my mouth, leaving a sweet taste. A person could get used to living this way. People at nearby tables talked about their day and seemed relaxed.

It was as if we'd forgotten for a time where we came from and why we had to leave.

As we were finishing dinner, an announcement came over the loudspeaker. "Ladies and gentlemen, we are now passing the Azores on the port side of the ship."

Chairs scraped back as people rushed out of the dining hall and onto the decks. Hannah and Ruth joined me and my family. The weather had turned again and there was a slight drizzle, but as we lined up along the port railing with the rest of the passengers, we saw the coast of one of the islands, so close we could make out the shapes of windmills through the mist.

Papa said, "Do you know what this means?"

He didn't give us a chance to answer. "We're almost halfway to Cuba."

13

MS *St. Louis*
Friday, May 19 – Saturday, May 20

HANNAH

I FELT DAVID close beside me at the rail while the sunset colored the misty coast of the Azores gold, then crimson. My skin prickled. I was super aware of everything, the breeze lifting the edge of my skirt and the orange light sparkling on droplets of mist in David's hair.

David said, "Papa told me there's really good birding on those islands. Too bad we won't be stopping there."

Eventually we lost sight of the Azores in the growing darkness. David and I walked down to D deck together. We stopped at the door of my cabin.

"So," David said, looking at his shoes. "Good-night. See you tomorrow."

Ruth had stayed on deck with her sailor, Hans. I read for a while. When the slight rocking motion of the ship made me sleepy, I turned out the light and said my prayers. As I had every night since leaving home, I prayed for Mother and Father to be

The Double Crossing

safe and join me soon in Cuba. Deep in my heart, though, I was afraid that even prayers couldn't help them.

I woke up sometime later to Ruth's sobs.

"Ruth, what's wrong?"

"I'm s-sorry I woke you." She turned on the light by her bed, sat up and blew her nose into her handkerchief. "What did I expect? It was just a shipboard romance. I'm Jewish and he isn't. It couldn't last."

"Ruth, you mean Hans? What happened?" I halfway sat up and tried to rub the sleep out of my eyes.

"I thought we had until the end of the trip." Ruth blew her nose again. "But he s-said he c-can't see me anymore. A steward, Otto Schiendick, is the *Ortsgruppenleiter*, the head Nazi on board. He told Hans he'd report him to the Party leadership if he kept 'fraternizing with a Jewess.' And he threatened him." She hiccoughed, "He said he'd be watching and if Hans was guilty of 'race defilement' he'd be in serious trouble. Then Hans told me he … he loves me. But there's nothing he can do." She broke down in tears again.

"Oh Ruth. I'm sorry. Can I get you something? A drink?"

"No. I'll be all right. It's just … I think I love him too." She covered her face with her hands and sobbed.

Schiendick again! That monster was nothing but trouble.

• • •

The next day, Saturday, announcements appeared on the bulletin boards telling everyone where Shabbat services were planned for that morning. There would be three separate services, because the passengers were from three different branches of Judaism. Ruth and I went to the Orthodox service in the social hall. Reform and Conservative services took place in other rooms.

As soon as we sat down, I noticed Hitler's portrait was gone.

Ruth's eyes were still red from crying the night before. She smiled. "Who do you think had the good taste to have that awful picture of Herr Hitler taken away?"

The quiet chatter of over a hundred people reminded me of a large flock of birds. I watched for David and his family, not expecting to see them. He'd told me they weren't religious. I kept thinking about him, and how close we'd stood the night before while we watched the sunset, sometimes our shoulders touched. What I did hear of the service wasn't very uplifting. The rabbi read from Hosea about adultery and fornication.

Before the rabbi finished, a commotion began in a kind of gallery above at the back. I turned to look. Schiendick was there, cursing at some crewmen who'd been watching the service. He didn't even bother to lower his voice as he practically dragged them out.

"That's him," I whispered in Ruth's ear. "Otto Schiendick. The chubby one. Remember we saw the captain stop him from singing that Nazi song?"

Ruth turned in time to catch a glimpse of the *Ortsgruppenleiter* leaving the gallery.

"Schiendick!" She spat the name as if getting rid of a bad taste. "I hate him."

I considered telling Ruth what else I knew about Schiendick. But it seemed like a bad idea. I wasn't sure Ruth could keep a secret.

14

MS *St. Louis*
Tuesday, May 23

DAVID

The ocean and sky seemed endless. We wouldn't see land again until we'd crossed the Atlantic. I stood at the rail with my binoculars, not actually thinking about birds, or Cuba. I'd been spending a lot of time with Hannah. Even when I wasn't with her, like now, I often thought about her. Most evenings we watched the sunset together, the water and heavens alive with color.

My family and everyone else seemed more relaxed now, from the gentle rocking of the ship, fresh ocean air, delicious food, and blue skies. Especially from knowing that we were heading to freedom, to a new life away from what we'd suffered in Germany.

I didn't like to think about Germany. No one talked about it now. We enjoyed three luxurious meals a day, played games, swam, or lay on lounge chairs reading, chatting and dozing. At night, we could go to movies, dances, or lectures. Anyone would think we were just a group of passengers on an ocean cruise.

The Double Crossing

• • •

Hannah and I took turns watching for Schiendick and reported to each other. But we didn't learn anything more about the spy plan. We saw him go in and out of the tourist class cabins. Once I watched him take a break, smoking and gazing out over the railing. He was alone, so no conversation to overhear. When I saw him finish his cigarette and flick the burning butt at a petrel flying below, I ground my teeth. He was hateful.

• • •

I was making other friends too, besides Hannah. I'd noticed the men with shaved heads the day we boarded the *St. Louis*. The ones who'd been in concentration camps. Today when I stood at the rail, thinking about Hannah and not really watching birds, one of those men came and stood next to me.

"I've noticed you with your binoculars. See anything interesting?" he asked.

"I'm mostly looking at birds. I've seen quite a few seabirds and learned a lot about them. My friend and I even got to take care of one for a few days when it hurt its wing."

"I'm Aaron Pozner," he said. "Mind if I look through your binoculars?"

"My name's David Jantzen. Go ahead." I handed them to him. "There's not much to see right now. I hope you don't mind me asking. I noticed your shaved head and my father told me that meant you'd been in a camp. My friend Hannah's father is in one of those. What was it like?"

"It was a nightmare. I was a Hebrew teacher outside of Nuremberg. On Kristallnacht, Nazis broke into my house and arrested me. They sent me to a camp called *Dachau*. I saw men murdered there. It happened every day. I was beaten several times."

That sounded terrible. I hoped Hannah's father was okay.

"One day I was released, with a group of other prisoners," Pozner went on. "They told us we had to leave Germany within fourteen days. The guards drove us to the train station in Nuremberg. My wife and two little children were waiting for me there. My family had raised money and she had my papers and a ticket for the *St. Louis*. She promised that she and the children would join me in Cuba as soon as possible."

He paused and swallowed. He wiped his eyes. "I didn't want to leave them. There was no money for another ticket. But I had to go, or they'd have arrested me again." A tear slipped out of his eye and he wiped it away. "Now it's up to me to earn the money and send for them, as quickly as I can."

Pozner's hair had started to grow out and I thought he'd probably put on some weight since being on the ship. Now that I knew his story, I realized what a load of sadness he was carrying.

• • •

Leo and I were also getting to be friends. He spent time with me when he could get away from his duties as the captain's steward. We talked about birds, and about Leo's experiences at sea. Sometimes he wanted to talk about Germany.

"Tell me more about what things are like in Germany. I've mostly been at sea recently. Why did you have to stay home after you couldn't go to school?"

"My parents didn't want us to go out. You never knew when you might run into gangs of Nazis or Hitler Youth." I didn't talk about this stuff much, but I trusted Leo. "They roamed around and randomly stopped people to ask questions. If you didn't wear the Nazi badge, or the badge of the *Deutsches Jungvolk*, the Hitler Youth, they might beat you up."

• • •

I didn't tell Leo what we'd learned about Schiendick. Later, when I talked to Hannah, she thought we should tell him.

"We could use his help. He can find out so much more about Schiendick than we can," she said.

The Double Crossing

"I know. We'll ask for his help if we have to. But think about it. Schiendick already has it in for Leo, and he has to go back to Germany on this ship. We don't want to get him in trouble with the Nazis."

She half-heartedly agreed. "Okay. For now."

Hannah and I were standing at the rail in the sunshine. The wind caught her hair, making it billow about her head like a circle of light. I was definitely starting to have more than just friendly feelings. I didn't know what to do about it. I'd never had a girlfriend.

"David! Look!" she shouted. "A whole cloud of birds flying over the water."

Cloud of birds was a good description. There must have been thousands in the huge flock coming toward us. She passed me the binoculars, and while I was scanning, trying to figure out what kind of birds were in the flock, Papa appeared at my shoulder, out of breath.

"Mama and I ... were walking around the deck ... when I saw them." He leaned on the rail, catching his breath.

"Are you all right, Papa?"

"Fine. I ran down ... to get my binoculars. And back up. Not as young as I used to be." He took another breath and smiled. "I hoped I'd find you. Wouldn't want you to miss this."

The flock wheeled and streamed, coming closer. Now we could see individual birds skimming the water, others diving under the surface.

"Mostly shearwaters," Papa said. "But I see some fulmars and petrels too. They're going to fly right by us."

"Oh, I hope none of them hit the ship and hurt themselves, like Peter did," said Hannah.

"Can you tell what kind of shearwaters they are, Papa?"

"Sooty Shearwaters, I think. I believe they're the only large, dark-colored shearwaters in the Atlantic. There must be a big school of fish, to attract so many birds. Here they come!"

The flock began to fly past the *St. Louis*, keeping only far enough from the ship to avoid hitting it.

"They glide right above the tops of the swells!" Hannah said.

The sun illuminated the water. I followed one of the birds as it ducked under the surface near the ship and swam, using its wings like oars.

"Are shearwaters tubenoses, Herr Jantzen?" Hannah asked.

"Yes. You're learning. They make one of the longest migrations of any bird, thousands of kilometers a year, and spend most of their lives at sea."

"Papa, Hannah, look!" I lowered the binoculars and pointed. "Dolphins, or maybe porpoises, a whole school, or pod, or whatever it's called."

The sleek animals rippled in and out of the water, swimming under the cloud of birds.

"Gosh!" Hannah said. "They're beautiful. There must be twenty or thirty of them."

Spellbound, we lost track of time. The birds seemed to go on forever. Then they disappeared, along with the dolphins, probably following the school of fish.

• • •

In the middle of the night, something woke me up. At first, I couldn't tell what was wrong. Then I realized the motion of the ship had changed. Shouts came from outside. It felt like the ship was changing direction. A bright light flashed past my porthole.

Rebekah was sleeping soundly in her berth, her breath slow and even. Quietly, I eased myself out of bed, pulled on my clothes, and crept from the cabin.

The deck was a buzz of activity. The ship seemed to be travelling in a circle. Some of the crew were in a launch down on the water, circling and calling out. Spotlights swept the sea near the small boat. Passengers and crew members hung over the rail, watching.

The Double Crossing

I found Leo and asked, "What's happening?"

He frowned. "One of the kitchen crew, a man named Leonid Berg, went overboard. Probably suicide. They're trying to find him."

My stomach lurched as I looked down, the height of a five-story building, to the black water. Sickened, I jerked back from the rail. "Why? Why would someone do that? Was he Jewish?"

"No. I mean, I don't think so. He was a crew member. Must have been downhearted. I hardly knew him." He lowered his voice. "A passenger died earlier in the day. Moritz Weiler, an old university professor. His wife says he died of a broken heart from having to leave his work and his country. The captain didn't want to upset the other passengers, so we had a small ceremony and burial at sea around 11:00 tonight. About an hour later, Berg jumped. From the same spot where they released Weiler's body."

The launch circled and searched for another hour, without finding the crewman. Three blasts on the horn called it back. The captain had given the order to resume our course for Cuba.

Passengers headed back to their rooms, some talking in low voices. I started back too, picturing the bodies of those two men, deep down under thousands of meters of cold, black water. A chill ran across my skin and I knew I was going to have nightmares.

15

MS *St. Louis*
Wednesday, May 24

HANNAH

Flocks of birds surrounded me in a flowing dance. Now I was a bird myself, winging with the flock across the ocean. I flew home to Oldenburg, searching for Father. I searched our home, the nearby *Schlossgarten* park, and the synagogue. I peered through the window of his jewelry shop where the name was painted: *Adam Coen Feiner Schmuck*. I couldn't find him. The glass was broken. Everything was ashes. I woke up, my cheeks wet with tears, and lay in bed a long time, missing my parents.

At breakfast everyone was talking about the sad news. A passenger had died the day before and been buried at sea during the night. Soon after, a crewman had committed suicide by jumping overboard. Some people in the dining saloon said they didn't think it was suicide. They said he got in a fight with the Nazis.

Herr Bergman, at a nearby table, said, "The crewman's name was Leonid Berg. He could have been Jewish. Maybe they dumped him over the side for that, or for being too friendly with the passengers."

The Double Crossing

The thought of it spoiled my appetite. Ruth and I looked at each other, alarmed.

"I heard he was a handsome young man who got 'romantically involved' with one of the Jewish girls," we heard a woman say. "He committed suicide when the Nazi watchdogs told him he had to give her up."

"Oh!" Ruth stood up and rushed out of the dining room. I followed her out on deck, where she clutched the rail, white-faced.

I touched her arm. "It wasn't him, was it? You said his name was Hans, not Leonid."

"No. But, it could have been." She began crying. "Oh! What kind of world is this? Why do people hate each other because of their religion?"

What could I say? All the horrible things that happened came rushing back. The awful teacher at school. *Kristallnacht*. The Nazis taking Father and then our house. I hung onto the rail myself, feeling sick and empty, with no comfort to give Ruth.

• • •

A special ceremony was scheduled for later that morning in the social hall to celebrate the first day of Shavuot, when God gave the Torah, the holy book, to the nation of Israel. Since Shavuot also celebrates the time of harvest in the Jewish homeland, the hall was decorated with bowls of fruit, vases of flowers, and two ornamental palm trees.

Ruth and I were lucky to find seats together in the crowded hall. I hoped the traditionally joyous celebration would take our minds off the deaths, at least for a while. And it did. Everyone who attended seemed more light-hearted afterward.

• • •

When we went in to lunch, Ruth said, "Do you mind if I join my friends again? I know I'm supposed to be your chaperone, but you seem to be doing just fine.

"Don't worry. I am. I'll eat with David and his family. There they are."

I said hello to the Jantzens and sat down to look at the menu. "Oh, wonderful, they're serving cheesecake. That's traditional for Shavuot. Did you go to the service?"

"No," said Rebekah. "Tell us about it, please."

"Fortunately, Herr Hitler wasn't glaring down at us. People said the captain had the portrait taken down again for services. They'd decorated the hall with bowls of fruit and flowers. It smelled so nice. The rabbi read from the Book of Ruth. That's traditional too, because Ruth was a convert to Judaism." I looked at David, kind of hoping he'd take an interest in the religion.

"Next time there's a service, I want to go," Rebekah said. "I hardly know anything about Jewish religion. Would that be all right, Papa?"

"I'm sorry I never introduced you children to the religion. I didn't grow up in a religious family myself, and don't know a lot about it. This is the first I've heard of this holiday. But Judaism is part of our heritage, and we've all been persecuted for that. We ought to know more about it."

"I agree," said Frau Jantzen. "Perhaps I'll go as well."

"Me too," David said. "To find out what it's all about, I mean. I don't think I'm going to start being religious."

"You'll have a chance tomorrow." I looked around the table. "It's the second day of Shavuot. There'll be another service in the social hall in the morning, if you want to come."

Religion had always been a big part of my life. Now it was the only thing I had left of my home and family. I wished I could share it with David. I was glad he wanted to learn about it.

• • •

After lunch David and I went on the deck with the binoculars, as usual. We stood looking at the cloudless sky and calm sea undulating past the ship, blue to the horizon. David seemed unusually quiet.

"What are you thinking?" I asked.

"About the man who went overboard. I woke up last night because of the lights and went on deck. The ship kept going in circles for about an hour, searching for him. I think the captain's trying to make up time now. You know, to stay ahead of those other ships."

I shivered. "Were you up when it happened?"

"No. After. I saw the lights and went on up to see what was going on. They had a boat in the water, and searchlights."

"What an awful thing," I said.

He grimaced. "Yeah. They never found him."

I shivered. Would the crewman have drowned in the cold, dark water? Or died from the fall?

We didn't say anything more for a while and were standing there quietly when Leo appeared. He gripped the rail, gritting his teeth.

"Leo, is something wrong?" David asked.

"I just came from Schiendick. Remember he wanted me to spy on the captain? Well, he cornered me in a first-class pantry and grilled me."

"What about?"

"Somehow, he found out that a few passengers met with the captain in his quarters yesterday. He wanted to know why I hadn't told him."

"Why were they meeting? What did you say?" I asked.

"The truth, mostly. A cable came from the HAPAG office. It said there may be a problem disembarking in Cuba."

"Oh, no!" My heart pounded. I felt a little dizzy.

"The captain asked the passengers he met with to form a committee, in case of trouble. I told Schiendick that, and when I saw how nervous it made him, I wanted to see him squirm. So I told him if there was trouble, the captain said he might cancel shore leave. He practically jumped out of his skin. I don't know why it's so important to him to go ashore in Havana. I doubt he's got a girl there." He gave a short bark of a laugh.

The situation wasn't funny, but Leo's nervous laugh released the tension. David and I couldn't help laughing too, at the idea of the obnoxious Schiendick with a girl in every port. Leo laughed harder and for a minute, no one could talk.

When I could catch my breath, I looked at David.

"Leo can help us. He can find out things we can't."

"Help you do what?" Leo asked. "Find out what?"

David started to shake his head, but it turned into a nod.

Checking to see no one was in ear shot, I lowered my voice. "We know why Schiendick is so keen to get ashore in Havana. We overheard him talking to one of his Gestapo men. He's a spy for the *Abwehr*. He's supposed to pick up secret U.S. military documents from someone in Havana and take them back to Germany."

"*Oh mein Gott! Der kleine Scheisser.* I'm not surprised."

"We plan to stop him. I wanted to tell the captain. But David—"

"I don't want to put Captain Schroeder, or you, in danger," David said. "You both have to go back to Germany. And you work for the Hamburg America Line. The Party controls HAPAG, right?"

"You're right about that, and about not telling the captain. He doesn't support the Nazis. But he loves his country. When it comes to military secrets, I think he wouldn't want to do anything to endanger Germany. In case we get into a war, that is. But I'll help. It's personal for me. Anything to stop Schiendick."

"Do you think there's going to be a war?" There was a quiver in David's voice.

"I don't know. There's a lot of talk."

I felt dizzy again. Mother and Father were still in Germany. If there was a war, they'd be in danger. *What if they can't get out to come to Cuba?*

16

MS *St. Louis*
Thursday, May 25

DAVID

As we neared the end of the trip, after ten days at sea, everyone got excited, full of energy, talking about plans for the future. Many passengers had family waiting in Cuba, or the United States, where, like us, they planned to go as soon as possible. Now on our tenth day at sea, we'd arrive soon. A costume ball was planned in the social hall, a tradition on the ship, two nights before landing.

At breakfast, Papa asked, "Shall we attend the service this morning? For the second day of Shavuot?"

"I want to go!" said Rebekah.

I nodded. I was curious. Besides, it meant more time with Hannah. I didn't know how or even if we'd get to see each other after we got to Havana.

I was disappointed when we arrived at the social hall for the service. Men and women sat on different sides. The make-shift synagogue was crowded. Papa and I found seats near the back on

The Double Crossing

the men's side, behind a sea of *yarmulkes*, the little round caps worn by religious Jewish men. Mama and Rebekah sat together on the women's side. Hannah's curly red hair was easy to spot near the front, but all I could see was the back of her head.

I kind of liked the service. Especially the chanting or singing parts. And I liked that it didn't last too long.

Afterward, Purser Mueller came on the loudspeaker telling passengers to report to his office to pick up landing cards for Saturday. It sounded like we would be getting off in Havana. For a moment I felt relieved. Maybe we didn't need to worry.

A long line stretched out the door of the purser's office and down the deck. Papa took one look. "Let's come back later. There's no rush."

I'd lost track of Hannah after the service. I kept searching for her, wanting to ask if she was going to the dance. I didn't know if I'd have the nerve to ask her to go with me, but maybe, if we started talking about it … I didn't have any idea what kind of costume I could put together. My hands felt cold and clammy even thinking about asking her.

• • •

When we walked into the dining saloon for dinner, the musicians were playing a familiar sounding waltz. I looked for Hannah, but didn't see her.

The dinner menu made my mouth water. Salmon mayonnaise, soup with dumplings, veal marengo with buttered noodles and roast potatoes or fried chicken with grilled tomatoes, cauliflower hollandaise, and chips. Orange ice cream for dessert.

While I was deciding what to order, Hannah appeared and asked to sit with us. At the sight of her, I felt so nervous about the dance that I lost my appetite. Things had been much easier when I'd thought of her only as a friend.

"I noticed you all came to Shavuot service this morning. What did you think of it?" she asked, sitting down next to me.

"I loved it," Rebekah said. "The flowers and the singing were beautiful. I like learning about being Jewish."

Mama said, "It was interesting to hear how the holiday celebrates God giving the people their holy book. Even though I'm not Jewish, I can appreciate the religion and history."

"We're all learning," Papa said. "It's ironic that Germany's treatment of us has brought us together as Jews."

"What about you, David? What did you think of the service?" Hannah's eyes were bright and hopeful.

"Um … I liked it. Especially the singing." It was hard to think clearly with the dance on my mind and her sitting next to me.

The soup arrived and we began eating, still talking about Shavuot and the Jewish religion. After I took a couple of swallows of soup, my appetite came back, and I focused on the food.

"So, David, are you going to the costume ball tonight?" Hannah looked at me, blushing.

I felt my color rise to match hers. "I, uh, don't know. I was thinking, maybe. Are you?"

"If you go, I will. Want to?" She smiled.

"Okay. But I don't know what to wear. Does everyone have to wear a costume?"

"It'll be fun to dress up and pretend. You could be a pirate. That's easy. Ruth has make-up. We can give you a beard and a scar. With an eye patch and a bandanna, you'll be perfect!"

"I want to go. Can I?" Rebekah looked at Mama.

"I don't know. People will be drinking, and it's going to last until late."

Papa said, "Let's let her come with us for an hour, and then to bed. And you, David, I don't want you to stay late either. I want you back in your cabin by ten-thirty."

Did they have to treat me like a kid? In front of Hannah?

"Oh, I wouldn't want to stay out any later than that anyway," Hannah said. "The next day we'll need to pack and get ready for Havana. We're supposed to arrive early in the morning, aren't we?"

The Double Crossing

"That's right," said Papa. "Before sunrise."

Soon we'll be in Cuba, I thought, starting a new life. I hoped Hannah would be a part of that life.

Rebekah and Hannah chattered on about costumes. I couldn't believe how easily it worked out to go to the dance together. And Hannah was going to come to our cabin to help me and Rebekah get ready.

• • •

I answered a knock on the cabin door an hour after dinner. Hannah twirled in, dressed as a gypsy, in a bright, full skirt and peasant blouse. She was barefoot and wore bracelets and beads. Colorful clothes, scarves, and bangles were draped over her arms. And she smelled like roses.

"Where did you get all this stuff?" Rebekah was riffling through the costumes even before Hannah finished setting them down on her bunk.

"I found a costume box in the library, for passengers to borrow. Here, David!" She held up an eye patch and a bandana. "For your pirate costume."

She had sailor pants for me and another bright colored skirt and blouse for Rebekah, as well as more bangles and beads.

"Oh, this is perfect," Rebekah held the skirt in front of her.

Hannah held up the pants for me. "I hope these fit you."

After Rebekah finished putting on her costume, I took a turn in the bathroom to change. I put on the pants and a shirt Hannah had brought. Once I was dressed, she tied the bandanna over my head.

"The pants are a little short." She stepped back. "But not bad." Pulling out an eyebrow pencil she'd borrowed from Ruth, she drew a scruffy beard on my cheeks. Her warm breath brushed my skin.

"Hold still," she said. "Stop smiling. You're messing it up!"

We both laughed. After she finished, Hannah examined her work and pulled the patch down over my eye. "You're perfect!"

Sylvia Patience

I could hardly breathe. She was standing right in front of me, smiling. I hoped the "beard" would hide my blush.

17

MS *St. Louis*
Thursday, May 25

HANNAH

My first dance! And with a boy I liked. David and I headed toward the social hall. I felt almost beautiful with my many-colored gypsy skirts and scarves floating around me and my bare feet padding on the deck. I floated in a cloud of the rose-scented perfume Ruth had dabbed on my wrists and temples. Everything was perfect. I was determined not to think about Schiendick, or any other worries.

Happy conversation filled the social hall and a band played dance music. Palm trees and flowers left from the Shavuot service were almost covered in colorful balloons. Streamers hung from the ceiling and gallery rails. Then I noticed the portrait of Hitler back in its place over the stage. I clenched my jaw.

"I see the Führer is back. He's glaring at us."

"Don't let it bother you. It's just a picture," David said.

He was right. I took a breath. I wasn't going to let that Nazi reminder spoil my evening.

Not everyone was wearing a costume. Some people had on formal evening dress. The women's long gowns clung to their hips and flared at the bottom, swirling beautifully with each turn of the dance. Some of the men in tuxedos were bare headed, their hair pomaded and neatly slicked to their heads. The more religious men still wore *yarmulkes*.

A lot of imagination went into costumes, pirates like David, and Arabs in bedsheets and bath towels. A couple of geishas minced by. Some of Ruth's friends were almost indecent as harem girls in bright flimsy see-through material.

Ruth herself hadn't come, saying, "I'm not in a party mood. And I don't want to run into you-know-who."

She shouldn't have worried. I didn't see any crewmen at the dance, although one woman wore a steward's uniform. I wondered how she got it.

We stopped at the bar to order apple drinks, then found seats at one of the little tables around the edges of the room. We drank our fizzy *Apfelschorle* while watching the dancers. I wanted to dance but my hands sweated at the thought of David and I holding each other and twirling around.

When the band began to play songs by the American bandleader Glenn Miller, some passengers clapped and cheered. I liked the swinging big band sound and my feet began tapping. The Nazis didn't approve of American music, but the style was so popular that they hadn't been able to stop people listening and it was even on the radio.

"I love this music," I said.

I thought David might want to dance. His foot was tapping too. But we just talked about the band and the costumes.

Cigarette smoke clouded the air. I caught sight of David's parents dancing. When the band started up the next piece, Herr Jantzen spun past with Rebekah standing on his shoes, giggling, and waving to us.

"That looks like fun!" I said.

"It does," David said, but he didn't take my hint. It looked like he wasn't going to ask me to dance before we had to leave. Even though I was nervous, I didn't want to miss out. It was my first dance. Finally, I took a breath and said, "Want to give it a try?"

"Dancing, you mean?"

I nodded.

His ears turned red and he cleared his throat. "I'm not very good."

"Me neither, but it looks like fun."

We got up and walked to the edge of the dance floor, trying not to bump into anyone. After a little embarrassed fumbling to figure out where to put our hands, we began to move in time to the music. At first, I looked down at my feet. David watched his shoes, careful not to step on my bare toes. But pretty soon we started to get the hang of it and let the music take us around. I laughed with the fun of it, and so did David. My feet glided across the smooth dance floor and my skirts rippled around us.

We danced to a couple more tunes, until the band started playing a tricky Latin rhythm. The audience clapped and whistled. A few couples broke into some showy dance steps. The women, and even the men, swung their hips, embarrassing me. I couldn't even look at David.

Soon after we sat back down, David's parents stopped at our table with Rebekah.

"We're going back to our room," Herr Jantzen said. "It's late and the rhumba's a little too fancy for us. Remember, don't stay out too long, you two."

We sat watching the dancers a little longer. A few people celebrating the end of the voyage apparently had too much to drink. My parents didn't drink, and I wasn't used to seeing grownups act foolish. When one couple stumbled, fell on the dance floor, and had to be helped back up, I was ready to leave.

"I should go. Tomorrow's a big day," I said. "Our last day on the ship."

Remembering what we'd heard about possible problems with landing in Cuba, I added, "I hope so, anyway."

David said, "Me too. I guess we kept ahead of those other ships. The ones we were trying to beat." We stood up together and went out on deck.

"Let's talk a minute before we go in," David said.

The night air was fresh after the smoky social hall. We naturally gravitated to the lifeboat where we'd hidden Peter. As we walked along the deck, we passed couples in the shadows between lifeboats. Some of them were kissing and I felt the heat rise to my face and the tips of my ears burned. David took my hand and my heartbeat sped up.

No one had taken "our" spot. I was still thinking of those couples kissing and feeling kind of romantic. David caught me off guard when he said, "I know I promised we'd try to figure out what to do about Schiendick before we get to Havana. But I don't think there's anything we can do. I mean, if we can't get help from the captain …"

I tensed and let go of David's hand. "We have to do something. Maybe go to the American embassy in Havana and tell them. Or maybe Leo can find a way to stop him. Oh! It's so important. I feel helpless!"

"I guess we could talk to Leo tomorrow. He might have an idea."

"All right," I said. "We'll talk to him, for a start anyway."

"Listen, Hannah," David's eyes went soft. "I … I want to see you in Havana. I really want us to stay in touch."

"I want that too. I won't know anyone there besides Ruth, and you and your family. You're like, my only friend."

He looked at me in such a tender way I had to remind myself to breathe.

We stayed a while, looking at the dark water reflecting the moonlight. I was a jumble of excitement over arriving in Havana, hope that David and I would still see each other, and worry over how to stop Schiendick. I forgot about kissing couples. I wasn't ready for that anyway. Finally, I said, "We'd better go get some sleep, to be ready for tomorrow."

David took my hand again and we walked back to the tourist class cabins. In spite of my worries, it had been a wonderful evening. I felt so light that, without his hand in mine, I might have floated away.

18

MS *St. Louis*
Friday, May 26

DAVID

When I woke up, Rebekah was still sleeping. I lay in my bunk for a while, thinking of the night before, the dance, and Hannah. Until, with a sinking feeling, I remembered that this was our last day aboard the *St. Louis*.

We were going to arrive in Havana in the very early hours of tomorrow morning. I was glad, of course, to be out of Nazi Germany and about to arrive in Cuba. And yet … this had been one of the best times of my life. I was sorry it was coming to an end.

Plus, things could still go wrong.

I'd agreed with Hannah that today, somehow, we'd try to find a way to stop Schiendick. Yes, I'd said I was in on it and I meant to keep my word. It was the right thing to do. But do what?

At breakfast, everyone talked about what fun the dance had been. Rebekah went on about the costumes. "And did you see that woman in the harem girl outfit? You could practically see through those bloomers she was wearing!"

The Double Crossing

"Hush, Rebekah," Mama said. "It's not polite to talk like that."

"Papa," I said. "How will we stay in touch with our friends, like Hannah, when we get to Cuba?"

"Make sure you get the address where she'll be staying." Papa cleared his throat. "And anyone else you want to keep in touch with. You can write when we know where we'll be. She's a lovely girl. But," he winked, "you're both a little young for romance."

I felt my face burn all the way to my scalp.

At that very moment, Hannah appeared. "Good morning Herr Jantzen, Frau Jantzen. Hi David and Rebekah. May I join you?"

I glared a warning at Rebekah not to say anything about 'romance.'

"Hi, Hannah." I stood up to pull out the chair next to me. "Please, sit down."

She sat and we exchanged a look that meant today's the day.

Mama asked, "Are you excited about arriving in Cuba tomorrow? Will someone be there to meet you?"

"Ruth and I are being met by a cousin of hers. We'll be staying with them."

I saw a mirror of my own confused feelings on Hannah's face. "I hadn't wanted to come on this voyage and leave my parents behind. But now I'm sad it's almost over. I didn't expect to make such a good friend." She smiled at me.

A warm glow rose in my chest. But Rebekah, that little tease, kept giving me sly looks.

As we were leaving the dining saloon after breakfast, Papa said, "We'd better pack our bags. We're supposed to bring them up on the deck this afternoon. David, Rebekah, be sure to lay out the clothes you'll wear tomorrow."

Rebekah followed our parents.

I exchanged a glance with Hannah.

"I'll be down to pack soon," I called after them.

Hannah and I went on the deck together. When we stood at the rail, I said, "It's gotten a lot warmer, hasn't it? The sky is so blue here." How dumb was that? I was talking about the weather.

"David," Hannah hesitated. "Are we …? I mean, are you …? Will we see each other in Cuba?"

I hated how easily I blushed. "Yes. We absolutely have to. We don't have an address yet. Some Jewish relief organization's going to help us. But if you give me the address where you're going to stay, I'll send you mine as soon as we do." I took her hand and squeezed it.

She squeezed back and smiled. "I'll get the address from Ruth and give it to you today."

We looked out at the ocean, bright blue like the intense sky, not saying anything for a few minutes. Then Hannah lowered her voice. "We still have Schiendick, and Operation Sunshine."

"I know. I hate to say it, but I think Leo's our best bet, if we can't ask the captain. Leo will have the whole trip back across the Atlantic to do something. But I don't like asking him to take the risk. Have you seen him since we told him about Operation Sunshine?"

"No. And I don't want to put him in danger. I still think we might have a chance to stop Schiendick from getting the information ourselves. If we watch him when we all get off the ship, maybe we'll see his contact and, I don't know, do something to keep him away, or grab the documents and run. Throw them in the ocean."

I raised an eyebrow. I admired her spirit, but it sounded more like comic book hero stuff than a plan.

"Well, maybe. I wouldn't count on having a chance. I like the idea you had about telling the American embassy. If we find out who his Cuban contact is, we can tell them that too."

We looked at the ocean in silence again for a while.

Hannah drummed her fingers on the rail. "I hate to say it, but I think you're right. Leo might be the only one who can keep the secret information from getting into the hands of the *Abwehr*. If we can't do anything before we get off the ship."

"I know. But how can we even ask him? And if we asked, I'm not sure he'd do it. I don't know if I would, in his place."

"Land!" someone shouted. Other excited voices followed.

The Double Crossing

An announcement came over the loudspeaker: "Ladies and gentlemen, the Florida coast is visible off the starboard side."

We rushed with the other passengers to the right side of the ship. Cheers went up all along the decks. We could see a distant, low lying coast. A strip of light-colored sand, and a line of trees behind it.

America! We'd crossed the ocean. I felt almost like an explorer. We cheered along with everyone else.

Hannah took off her sweater. "It's getting so warm and humid. If it weren't for this breeze, it would be hot." The wind lifted her curls. Without thinking, I smoothed her hair. She smiled at me. I grinned back, embarrassed.

• • •

After lunch, I was back at the rail on the B deck with my family. Now we could see buildings along the coast.

"That must be Miami," someone said.

Word spread down the line of passengers. Cheers went up again. Several people rushed away.

"Where are they going?" I asked Papa.

"The man next to me said he was going to the purser's office to send a telegram to relatives in Cuba, letting them know we're arriving."

• • •

I finally caught sight of Leo that afternoon, hurrying from one place to another, unable to stop and talk. It looked like we would have to wait until after dinner.

Dinner was scheduled early so passengers could get to bed. The *St. Louis* would arrive in Havana before dawn. Rebekah and I took our bags up to the deck before we went to the dining saloon.

Hannah joined us at the table. "Ruth's eating with her friends one last time." She kept giving me worried looks and didn't make her usual easy conversation with Rebekah and my parents.

After dinner, the two of us went on the deck together again. Hannah said, "This may be our last chance. We have to find Leo and ask him."

"I kept trying to talk to him all afternoon, but he's been so busy."

"Me too. Every time I saw him, he was in too much of a hurry to stop."

We decided to try to corner him by the stairs to the bridge deck. We waited there until we saw him coming down from the captain's cabin.

"Leo," I said, "we have to talk to you."

"For just a minute. I'm running an errand for the captain."

We pulled him to a quiet spot and huddled close.

Hannah whispered, "It's about Schiendick. We wanted to ask you if, that is, if we aren't able to stop him from getting you-know-what from his contact in Havana. I mean, we're going to try. But, if we can't … would you … try to find it and get rid of it? On the way back?"

"We know it's a big risk for you," I said. "We didn't want to ask. But … we're not sure we'll have any other way to stop him."

"If it comes to that, I'll do what I can." Leo lowered his voice. "If the Nazis are planning to make war, I don't want them to win. But," he frowned, "Schiendick may not be able to meet his contact."

"What?" Hannah said.

"Why not?" I asked.

"The captain had a wireless from the HAPAG office in Havana. It said to anchor out in the harbor, not to make any attempt to go alongside the dock."

Leo's worried tone was as troubling as his words. My dinner churned in my full stomach.

"Is that normal?" Hannah said. "Maybe it's just their procedure."

"I don't think so. The captain is very concerned."

Part Two

19

MS *St. Louis*, Havana Harbor
Saturday, May 27

HANNAH

I SAT STRAIGHT UP IN BED. The ship's horn gave another loud blast. That was what had woken me up. Bleary eyed, my heart racing, I turned on the bedside light and squinted to read the little clock. Four in the morning. Leo said we were supposed to anchor out in the harbor!

I looked over at Ruth. She stirred, muttered something, and pulled the blankets up over her head. I didn't want to wake her. The night before we'd stayed up late talking about our new lives in Cuba, too excited to fall asleep. I hadn't told her about the captain's orders not to tie up at the dock. Maybe it was normal for Cuba. No reason to upset her, yet.

I dreaded having to say good-bye to David and his family. I felt almost as lost and alone as when I left Mother in Hamburg. How was it that in only two weeks I'd come to care so much about them?

I scrambled out of my bunk, dressed, and went up on deck.

By starlight and a sliver of moon, I made out the distant shoreline, some white buildings, occasional car headlights. The warm, humid air smelled of a complicated mixture of gasoline, garbage, and flowers.

The engines chugged as the ship made slow progress through the harbor. What would Cuba be like? It would be exciting to learn Spanish words, a whole new language. Other passengers joined me on deck, talking in hushed, animated voices.

At 4:30 the breakfast gong sounded. The tourist class dining saloon was already full of talking, laughing passengers. Many wore their best clothes for landing. Some of the women's hats were cocked at carefree angles and decorated with flowers, feathers, or veils.

David and his family were at their usual table.

"Good morning," Frau Jantzen said. "Please join us."

"Aren't you excited?" Rebekah was bouncing a little in her seat. "Today we're going to get off the ship. We're in Cuba!"

"Of course." I hoped it was that simple. I saw a small crease appear in David's brow.

Soon after we began eating, the ship's motion stopped. At the grating sound of the anchor chain, we rushed to the windows where we could see lights on shore, still a long way off.

I exchanged a look with David. We were anchored far from the docks.

Gradually everyone sat back down to finish breakfast. Now people sounded anxious, wondering out loud why we'd anchored in the middle of the harbor. A man at the next table said, "They raised the yellow quarantine flag. We'll probably have to stay out here until the medical authorities say we can land. A routine procedure, I expect."

Maybe that was it. Probably every ship coming into the Havana harbor had to be inspected. But I kept thinking: Leo said the captain was worried.

• • •

We went on deck after breakfast, along with most of the passengers. The sky began to lighten, though the sun wasn't up yet. Ruth and I stood along the crowded rail with David and his family, looking at the shore and the harbor. Now we could see the narrow harbor entrance the ship had come through in the dark, guarded by what looked like a castle with turrets. Further in, the harbor widened and splayed out into several channels, like fingers of a hand, surrounded by buildings and houses rising up onto hills.

Rebekah took my hand, bouncing with excitement. "Hey, Havana! Hannah in Havana."

Everyone laughed. I said, "That's right! Very clever."

I leaned close to David. "Watch for Schiendick, in case he leaves, or his contact comes on board."

He nodded, then turned at the sound of a launch approaching the *St. Louis*.

The ship's doctor, Dr. Glauner, was waiting at the top of a foldable metal stairway the crewmen called the accommodation ladder. It was the same gangway we'd come up when we boarded, but now the stairs hugged the side of the ship, ending at a platform on the water. Cuban policemen stood guard, one on the lower platform and two more at the top. They must have come on board while everyone was at breakfast.

The launch pulled up to the platform and a man in a white suit and hat stepped off, spoke briefly to the officer at the bottom, and climbed the stairway. Dr. Glauner greeted him and led him toward the bridge.

"That will be the Port Authority doctor," David's father said. As soon as he clears us, I expect we'll be able to dock and disembark."

"Wonderful," Frau Jantzen said. "It's been lovely, but I'm ready to get off this ship."

I hoped he was right. Maybe Leo worried too much. David, standing next to me, secretly slid his hand into mine and smiled down at me. The skin of my palm tingled where we touched.

On the A deck the ship's orchestra began playing, *Freut euch des Lebens*. Some of the words were, "Be happy you're alive." People smiled, swaying to the music, or singing along.

People along the deck started moving away. Soon the purser and the ship's nurse came up to us and asked us to line up in the social hall. "The port doctor wants to see everyone in person."

We followed the others and joined a long line waiting to enter the social hall. Even though it was early, the day was beginning to heat up.

"Why don't they take us in groups?" Ruth whispered. "Instead of making everyone swelter in the sun in this cursed line."

Eine Warteschlange. One of my favorite words. A line like a snake. Well, I liked the word, but I didn't like the thing itself.

Inside the social hall at last, we approached the doctors and some other uniformed officers seated behind a table, checking lists of passengers' names. By now everyone was sweating and grumbling about the delay.

When it was my turn, an officer asked for my name and found it on a list.

"Do you have a cough, skin rash, or any contagious disease?" the Cuban doctor asked through an interpreter.

"No."

"Are you sound of mind and body?"

"Yes."

I expected more, maybe some sort of examination, but that was it. Ruth and I made our way through the crowd leaving the social hall and back on deck.

"What was the point of that?" David asked, as he and his family joined us. A little breeze stirred the humid air.

"I don't know," I said. "All that waiting in the heat for a couple of questions. What do they expect people to say? By the time we got there, I felt like telling them I had a rash all over my body. I probably do, from the heat."

Ruth and David laughed. Rebekah giggled.

"Good thing you didn't say that," David said. "They might have sent you back to Germany."

That sobered us all.

When the others went down to gather up their things, I took David's arm and pulled him back to the rail.

"At least one of us has to stay to watch for Schiendick."

"Oh! There he is!" David pointed.

The Nazi steward leaned on the rail next to the accommodation ladder, watching another launch approach. It flew the HAPAG flag.

"Look!" I hissed, "See that man in the boat? Maybe he's the one."

The man climbed the ladder to the deck, puffing and red faced in the heat. He straightened his white suit, took off his hat, and wiped his forehead with a handkerchief. Schiendick stepped in front of him and said something.

The man from the boat asked Schiendick something, then raised his voice angrily. "Robert Hoffman? He's my assistant. He has no business on board the ship. If you want to see him, you'll have to go ashore."

"David! Did you hear? Robert Hoffman must be the name of his contact. And he must work for HAPAG."

"Make yourself useful, steward," the man bellowed. "Bring the mail bag up from the boat."

Schiendick took a step back, his face red, but he did as he was told.

Mail! My heart raced with excitement. There might be a letter from Mother, perhaps news of Father.

"Will you watch?" I asked David. "I want to check the mail."

"Sure. I'll stay right here. I hope you got a letter, but don't worry if you didn't. Letters have to cross the ocean too."

20

MS *St. Louis*, Havana Harbor
Saturday, May 27

DAVID

Hannah came back without a letter, disappointed, her face flushed. Tears shone in her eyes.

"It's so hard, not knowing what's happening to my parents."

"I'm sorry you didn't get a letter. Probably the mail will catch up with us soon."

She fidgeted at the rail for a few minutes, like a nervous bird, wiping her eyes frequently.

"I need to go to my cabin and lie down for a while," she said, her voice cracking. "Do you mind watching? In case Hoffman shows up."

"Sure. Don't worry. I'll be right here."

The harbor teemed with birds, some I'd never seen before. But all I could think about was Hannah and how sad she seemed. I couldn't imagine what it was like for her to leave her parents in Germany and not hear from them.

Finally, a couple of huge black birds with forked tails caught my attention. They hovered on the wind overhead. One had a

The Double Crossing

white collar, the other a red pouch below its neck. Their wingspan must have been over two meters and they soared like kites. What were they? I lowered the binoculars. Papa would know.

Passengers lined the rails, watching the shore and complaining about the delay. I looked from one group to another until I spotted my father with Rebekah not far away and hurried to them.

"Papa! Look." I pointed. "See those birds? Here, take my binoculars. Do you know what they are?"

He took the binoculars and focused on the birds. "Beautiful!" Handing them back, he said, "They're Magnificent Frigate birds. I recognize them from books. The males have that red pouch during breeding season. That's a new bird for both our life lists."

"I'm so hot!" Rebekah whined, not like her usual cheerful self. She tilted her head up. Her hair hung limp and damp. Sweat beaded on her forehead.

Papa said, "Come on, *liebchen*. Let's go find your friends. You should go for a swim. It's too hot to stand out here."

"David, after I get your sister out of this heat, I'll go see if I can find out what's going on. It's outrageous that they're making us wait like this, in the middle of the harbor. Do you want to come?"

"I'll stay to see what's going on. I'm okay."

On shore, a crowd was gathering near the docks. Small boats began to surround the *St. Louis*. The man from HAPAG left in his launch.

Time dragged by and the heat was starting to bother me too. My head throbbed and sweat dripped down my back. When Hannah came back up, her eyes were puffy, like she'd been crying. I wished there was something I could do to help.

"Are you all right?" I asked.

"I will be," she said.

"Nice hat," I said, noticing the wide brimmed hat she was wearing, thinking what a dumb thing that was to say when she was so unhappy.

"To keep the sun off my face." She touched my hot cheek and it felt even hotter. "You should wear one too."

Standing watch wasn't so bad now that Hannah was with me. "Look!" she pointed. "Isn't that the HAPAG launch again?"

Sure enough, the launch was returning.

"Why are they back? They just left," I wondered out loud.

A different man climbed from the launch onto the lower platform. He also wore a white suit and hat. It seemed they all wore white. It made sense with the heat. The man spoke to the policeman on the lower platform, too far down for us to hear. The policeman blocked him from coming up. The man tried to hand the officer a carved walking stick and a bundle of magazines he carried. The policeman refused, blocking his way and shaking his head.

The man turned and yelled up at the ship, "Otto Schiendick!"

"He's calling for Schiendick." Hannah said. "I bet it's his contact! Hoffman."

I looked around for Schiendick. He wasn't at the top of the ladder anymore.

Below, the policeman put his hand on his gun holster, threatening the man, who turned and got back in the boat.

"You're right. It's the HAPAG launch. It must be him," I whispered. "The other man said he works there."

As the boat sped away, Schiendick hurried across the deck. He stared after the launch and asked another steward who stood by the stairway, "Is that Herr Clasing from HAPAG going back to shore?"

"It was another man. He called out for you. Didn't you hear him? He told the policeman his name was Hoffman."

"That was him," I whispered.

Schiendick pounded his fists angrily against the railing, then gripped it and leaned out. I caught my breath. He looked like he was going to jump into the harbor. But he turned and stomped away.

"Hoffman was trying to give that walking stick and magazines to the policeman," Hannah whispered. "The information could be hidden in them."

The Double Crossing

"I bet you're right." Hannah would make a good detective.

"Maybe Schiendick won't be able to get the documents and we won't have to do anything," she said.

"That would be great, but I doubt they'll give up that easily."

Another launch sped up to the landing platform, this one flying the Cuban flag. A group of men in uniforms and more Cuban policemen got out and came aboard the *St. Louis*. A babble of conversation went through the watching passengers, sounding like a flock of geese.

"They're customs and immigration officials," was the news spreading through the crowd.

Hannah said. "This all seems like normal procedures for us to land, don't you think?" She didn't look convinced.

I wasn't sure either. "Maybe. I guess."

• • •

We heard yelling from below and looked down again. Men stood up in the rowboats that had clustered on the port side of the ship. They were offering fruit for sale. Passengers yelled back and forth with the vendors. Some of the fruits were familiar to me, like bananas and pineapples. Others I didn't recognize. One kind looked like a giant grapefruit and another was small and brown.

Policemen began passing fruit up the accommodation ladder. Passengers and crew members took the fruit and passed money back down.

More boats arrived beside the *St. Louis*. People called names up to the ship. Several passengers recognized relatives in the boats.

"There he is! There!" One mother kept shouting and pointing as her young daughter tried to see where her father was.

Passengers on the ship jumped up and down, waving, and crying in their excitement.

"At last, we're among friends," someone called in a high voice that pierced the hubbub.

Papa worked his way through the crowd to join us at the railing. "The immigration officers are processing passengers. They're starting with first class, but be ready. I have your passport and papers, David. Do you have yours with you, Hannah?"

"Yes, thank you. So, you think we'll be getting off the ship soon?"

"It looks that way. Maybe they'll take us ashore in the launch, one group at a time."

I relaxed at the news. Hannah smiled and I could almost see the tension leave her.

After Papa left, Hannah frowned. Her worried look returned. "David, we've got to tell Leo about Hoffman, before we get off the ship. If they don't let him come on board, Schiendick might go ashore. Leo needs to know about the magazines and the walking stick."

"All right." I had to agree, though I wished we could just forget about Schiendick and his scheme.

"When we get to shore, we'll warn the Americans too, now that we know the name of the agent here," Hannah said.

• • •

Passengers filed in and out of the first-class saloon. By 10:30, about fifty people had collected their hand luggage and were standing near the accommodation ladder, waiting for a boat to take them ashore. The day was an oven. I wiped sweat from my forehead. It dripped inside my clothes. Hannah's face was flushed even under her hat. I'd never felt such a damp heat in Hamburg. Or such a blazing sky. And it was still morning.

The group of passengers near the ladder began pointing excitedly. The Cuban government launch was returning. It tied up to the landing platform. An officer jumped out and ran up the metal stairs. He ignored the waiting passengers and went straight to the dining saloon. Minutes later, he returned, followed by all the Cuban officials. They hurried past the group of passengers, down the accommodation ladder, and sped away in the launch.

The Double Crossing

People stared after them in stunned silence. The only Cubans remaining behind on the *St. Louis* were the policemen.

An irritated buzz of questions rose among the first-class passengers waiting to leave.

"Aren't we going ashore after all?" asked a child nearby.

"Hush! I don't know," his mother said.

People complained angrily. A few started to cry.

• • •

"There he is!" Leo was coming down the stairs from the bridge deck. Hannah and I had been looking for him since after lunch. I took Hannah's hand and we hurried to catch him.

"What's happening?" Hannah asked as soon as we caught up with him. "Are they going to let us land?"

Leo led us to a quiet spot. "The captain's worried. No one's telling him anything. He said all he could get out of the head policeman was that things go slower in Cuba. But do you remember those other ships I told you about? The ones with more Jewish refugees?"

Hannah and I looked at each other. Her wide eyes reflected my own worry. We both nodded.

Leo pointed to a smaller ship anchored some distance from us. "That's one of them. The *Orduña*. It just arrived.

"And I overheard the captain brief his officers over lunch today. He told them he'd set up a passenger committee, as a way to communicate with the passengers. Some of the officers didn't like the idea. They said it gave the Jews too much status. The captain's answer was, 'We aren't in Germany now. I won't tolerate the kind of attitude toward these people that they experienced at home.'"

"We're lucky Captain Schroeder is our captain." Hannah said what I was thinking. "They could have put a Nazi in charge."

"That's right. I think the committee is a good idea," I said. "We need to know what's happening."

"We get daily radio reports from Germany," Leo said. "They keep talking about bad feelings among the Cubans toward Jewish refugees.

The captain said it might be typical propaganda, but if it's true, things could get unpleasant. He cancelled shore leave for the crew."

"Good!" said Hannah. "Schiendick won't be able to meet Hoffman."

"Hoffman?" Leo said.

"His contact," I said. "We saw him try to come on board. The policeman wouldn't let him. His name's Robert Hoffman."

"He works in the HAPAG office," Hannah burst in before I could finish, "If Schiendick gets the documents from Hoffman after we get off the ship, it will be too late for us to do anything. If that happens, do you think you could look for the documents and destroy them?"

Leo's brow creased. "Well, I …"

Hannah didn't wait for him to finish. "We think they're hidden in some magazines and a walking stick Hoffman was carrying."

"We don't want to put you in danger," I hurried to add. "But, if you have the chance?"

"Purser Mueller told the captain he might have trouble from Schiendick," Leo said, not answering our questions. "He keeps asking when he can go ashore. But there's one bit of good news."

"Really? What?" I couldn't imagine.

"The captain said if things don't work out in Cuba, he's confident the United States will accept all of you as refugees."

The United States was where my family wanted to go anyway.

Hannah's eyes lit with hope. "Thanks for telling us, Leo. But what do you say? If Schiendick gets the documents after we leave, will you try to take them? I mean, we haven't given up. But will you, if we can't?"

I smiled a little to myself. When Hannah was on a mission, nothing distracted her.

Leo frowned. "I'll do what I can. But I'm a bit afraid of him. I mean, if it was just him … but he has his Gestapo squad. If they caught me, I wouldn't put it past them to throw me overboard. Make it look like suicide, like that Berg fellow from the kitchen."

The Double Crossing

A chill snaked up my spine. "Is that what happened to him?" I felt even worse now, asking Leo to take such a risk.

"No. I don't know. I'm just saying, it's easy to assume a 'man overboard' is a suicide when it could be murder."

• • •

All afternoon passengers milled about the decks, watching the harbor and docks for any change. The crowd on shore had grown to hundreds. Passengers' relatives came out in all kinds of boats. A throng of them surrounded the ship, like baby ducklings around their mother.

I spotted the *Orduña* heading to the docks. "Look, Hannah!"

Other passengers pointed and commented.

"Why are they being allowed to dock before us?" an angry woman's voice rose over the others. "We were here first."

"Calm down," said the man next to her. "They're a smaller ship, fewer passengers. It's a good sign. We'll be docking soon too."

I didn't feel as hopeful.

The watching passengers continued to ask questions, grumble and complain. They wiped sweat off their faces with handkerchiefs and fanned themselves with paper fans.

Hannah looked wilted. When she took off her hat to fan herself, her normally curly hair was a tight, damp frizz. After a while, when nothing else happened, she said, "I'm going back to my cabin for a while. How about you?"

"I'll stay for now. Just in case there's something to see."

Papa came on the deck. I caught up to him as he was crossing to the accommodation ladder.

"Any news?" I asked.

"They still aren't telling us anything! I want to see if that policeman knows what's going on."

I followed Papa. He asked the Cuban policeman, using the little Spanish he knew, when the *St. Louis* would be allowed to dock.

The policeman's only answer was, "*Despues de Pentecostes.*"

"What did that mean?" I asked Papa as we walked away to stand at the rail again.

"I think it was, 'After Pentecost.'"

"What's that?"

"It's a Christian holiday. Maybe they take a long weekend."

"That's not fair! They make us wait here and don't tell us anything! What kind of government is that?"

"Have patience, son. At least it's not a Nazi government."

I flushed. "I want to have patience, but it's too hot! I'm sick of waiting."

"Everyone's feeling that way, son. I'm going below to get out of this heat. You should too."

Papa left and I was about to go below too when another launch came alongside. A man in uniform climbed the accommodation ladder. What now?

The man was escorted to the bridge deck. I'd decided again to go below when an announcement came over the loudspeaker asking several passengers to report to the purser's office. Curious, I decided to wait a while longer to see what would happen. Not long after, a small group of passengers was escorted to the launch.

A man nearby said, "At least four of them are Cubans. I saw them get on in France."

"But I recognize that woman and her children," another man said. "They're German. Jews, like us. Why are they letting them off?"

Crewmen handed down suitcases, and the launch left, carrying the group to the dock.

I did the numbers in my head. Seven passengers just got off. One had died. That meant there were still 929 passengers waiting on the *St. Louis*.

As I watched the launch pull away, I noticed passengers on the *Orduña* were disembarking. I looked through my binoculars. The passengers headed down the gangway and were greeted by people on shore. Their bags were off-loaded and piled on the dock.

The Double Crossing

The *Orduña* was supposed to be carrying Jewish refugees too. What was going on? Surely if they'd been allowed to land, we would be too. But then why had it been so important for the *St. Louis* to get here first?

In spite of the heat, I stayed on the deck to watch, determined to know what was happening. No one else came or went from the *St. Louis* the rest of the afternoon. But just before I went to dinner that evening, the *Orduña* sailed past on her way out of the harbor, the British flag flying from her stern. Passengers clung to her rails, leaning out and looking back toward the docks.

So not all of them had disembarked. Why? What did it mean?

21

MS *St. Louis*, Havana Harbor
Sunday, May 28 – Monday, May 29

HANNAH

When Ruth and I left the cabin to go to breakfast, the bright sun was already glaring in the sky and the heat and humidity were intense. It wasn't possible to feel clean. I'd just showered and already I was sweaty and sticky.

I joined the Jantzens at their table. The only conversation was Rebekah's hopeful question.

"Papa, will we get off the ship today?"

"I hope so, my love."

Most of the passengers in the dining saloon ate in silence or talked in low voices. I couldn't follow their conversations, but people sounded angry, and worried. One woman broke into tears. The sour, fearful smell of sweaty bodies made me anxious.

David wore a cap with a bill and his face was sunburned from the day before. Occasionally he lifted a bite to his mouth. He glared at his plate and seemed lost in thought. His binoculars hung from the back of his chair. Most of the food on his plate was still untouched when he asked, "May I be excused to go on the deck?"

When he stood up, I said, "I'm going too. I mean, please excuse me," and followed.

The only thing different when we looked toward shore was that another ship, smaller than the *Orduña*, had docked. It flew a French flag, and its name, painted near the bow, was *Flandre*.

I recognized the name. "That's the other refugee ship Leo told us about! I don't see anyone going ashore."

David looked through the binoculars, then handed them to me. A group of people had gathered on the quay next to the ship, talking and gesturing back and forth with those on the deck. A woman leaned over the rail and blew kisses to a man below.

"Why did they let the other ships dock and not us? I don't understand."

"I don't know," David said. He sounded discouraged.

"Let's look at birds while we wait to see what happens." I hoped that would cheer him up.

It kept getting hotter, with little breeze to stir the thick air. Even so, for a while we were able to forget everything but birds. We took turns with the binoculars. David pointed out grebes and shearwaters. While he watched a small grebe through the binoculars, I caught sight of a flock of large pink birds flying across the water.

"Oh, pink birds! David, what are those?"

He turned to where I pointed and raised the binoculars. "Flamingos! I've seen pictures. Quick, take the binoculars."

The birds were bright orange-pink, their wings outlined in black. Long necks stretched out in front as they flew, and equally long legs stretched behind.

"Gosh! I've never seen anything like that." I handed the binoculars back to David.

"Their color comes from the shellfish they eat. I've read about it."

When the flamingos were out of sight, loud squawking in the distance from the ever-present gulls drew our attention. Several of the birds were fighting over scraps on the dock, making a terrible racket.

"Gulls are the same everywhere, greedy and quarrelsome," David said.

"Like Nazis."

He snorted a contemptuous laugh. "Right. Just like Nazis."

"Oh, see those!" He pointed to a pair of enormous birds overhead. "Those are Magnificent Frigate birds. Probably the same ones I saw yesterday."

It was like watching kites gliding. They hardly moved their wings. "I wish we could soar like that, away from all this worry and misery. Don't you?"

When we couldn't stand the heat any longer. David said. "Nothing's happening. Let's unpack our bathing suits and go to the pool."

Swimming helped my mood. David seemed to relax too. Every once in a while, one of us went to the rail to check on the *Flandre*, still at the dock, and to watch for Hoffman, in case he came back. People crowded around the smaller ship, but no one got off. Finally, I went to my cabin to shower and take a nap.

When I woke, it was evening. After dressing for dinner, I went up to the A deck to stand at the rail. I didn't see David. I didn't feel like talking, anyway. The anxious mood on board weighed me down. There went the *Flandre*, sailing toward the mouth of the harbor. Passengers lined the small ship's rails. It didn't look like anyone had been allowed to land. My stomach tightened. Would we be made to leave too?

• • •

The next day was Monday. David and I took turns keeping watch on the deck all morning to give each other breaks from the heat. Nothing happened.

We were together on deck in the afternoon when another launch approached the *St. Louis* with a uniformed Cuban policeman and a man in the typical white suit. He held his hat with one hand to keep it from blowing away, as the boat sped toward us. When the men came on board, Captain Schroeder met them at the top of the accommodation ladder. At once they were surrounded by a crowd of curious passengers, Cuban police, and crew members. Everyone was hungry for news. David and I got as close as we could to the new arrivals.

The captain spoke to the policeman, then introduced himself to the other man, who was tall, slim, and neatly dressed, his hat still in place.

"I'm Dr. Max Aber. I've come to pick up my daughters," he said in German.

Captain Schroeder replied, "You've been authorized to take them."

A woman brought two little girls straight from the pool, water dripping from their bathing suits. The father cried and hugged the girls, who seemed shy and unsure. "I've missed you so much."

Tears came to my eyes. Dr. Aber reminded me of my own father.

The woman took the girls back to dress and collect their things. After Captain Schroeder left, passengers pushed in around Dr. Aber, all talking at once and asking questions.

"What's going on in Havana?"

"Can you help us?"

"When can we get off the ship?"

Dr. Aber raised his voice over the crowd, and they quieted to listen. "I'm sorry. I don't know. The situation with the *St. Louis* is very political. Articles in the paper. Even people protesting against more Jewish refugees—"

"How were you able to get your girls?" interrupted one of the passengers.

Aber looked nervously at the hot, sweaty passengers surrounding him. "They have proper visas, not those landing permits that Manuel Benitez sold everyone."

At that the crowd erupted.

"Benitez? Isn't he the Director of Immigration?"

"What's wrong with our landing permits?" a woman shouted, sounding almost hysterical. Others repeated her question.

Dr. Aber raised his voice to make himself heard again.

"Benitez used a loophole. The landing permits are supposed to be for tourists. He made a lot of money selling them. The Cuban president is angry. The loophole's been closed. At the beginning of the month the government passed Decree 937, like the number of passengers on this ship. Benitez' landing permits are now invalid for refugees."

"Wait a minute!" One of the men near the back of the group shouted. "They passed it at the beginning of the month? Before we sailed?" His face was flushed. "Why didn't anyone tell us?"

Many of the other passengers repeated the man's question. People sounded angry.

I felt dizzy. This must be why the HAPAG office warned the captain we might have trouble landing.

Dr. Aber said, "I'm sorry. I don't know. The refugee organizations are trying to get the President to allow you to land. But the Cuban people are stirred up against taking in more refugees. Please. There's still hope. Others have been allowed in."

The crowd dissolved into smaller groups, talking heatedly and complaining. Several women broke down crying.

"After all the hints we've had, I shouldn't be surprised," David said, leaning close. "But on top of everything, now it turns out we've been swindled by this Benitez. That really makes me mad!"

"I'd like to know why even Captain Schroeder didn't know about this, if that law was passed before we left," I whispered.

"It's beginning to look like our only hope is for Captain Schroeder to take us to the United States," he said.

• • •

The Double Crossing

The two little girls returned, dressed in frilly party dresses. Dr. Aber hugged each one again, passed their suitcases down, then helped the girls down the stairs to the platform. As the launch sped away, the children waved to the watching passengers. Some waved back.

"Two more gone. Now there are 927 of us," David said.

"They're lucky girls," I said, "getting off the *St. Louis*, and united with their father." *If only my father could come for me.*

Another two boats sped toward the ship, each carrying an official looking man. I recognized the second of the boats as the HAPAG launch. David raised his binoculars.

"It's Hoffman! But he isn't carrying anything."

"What's he doing here, then?"

The first boat docked, and a man climbed the ladder.

"My name's Milton Goldsmith," he announced to the Cuban policeman stationed at the top. "I'm with the Jewish relief organization. I have a meeting with the passenger committee."

As a crewman was leading him off to his meeting, Hoffman's launch docked. This time he was allowed to come aboard. As soon as he reached the deck, Leo appeared. "Captain Schroeder will see you in his cabin. Follow me please."

"Why does the captain want to see him?" I despised the *Abwehr* agent. *He must have some scheme to get the secret papers to Schiendick.*

"He works in the HAPAG office. Remember? They own the ship."

"Do you think he'll try to pass the documents to Schiendick?" I asked.

"He didn't have anything with him this time. So probably not. He must be here for another reason." David leaned closer. "I'd love to know what goes on in that passenger committee meeting."

That gave me an idea. "I bet they're meeting in the social hall. C'mon. We can sneak onto the balcony. They'll never know we're there." I took David's hand and pulled him along.

Crouched in the balcony of the social hall, David and I listened as Mr. Goldsmith gave the committee a depressing report.

"I'm Milton Goldsmith with the Jewish Relief Organization here in Havana. A couple of representatives of the American Jewish Joint Distribution Committee, or the Joint as we call it, are on their way here to pressure President Bru's government to let you in. But the outlook is grim."

He went on to say that a lot of politics were involved. There was a feud between President Bru and Benitez over the landing permits.

"And," he said ominously, "the Cuban newspapers have picked up German propaganda against Jews. Public opinion opposes us."

My mouth felt dry. So, the Cubans hated us like the Germans did. My jaw hurt and I realized I was clenching it. David reached for my hand and squeezed it. I didn't dare say anything, even whisper, for fear we'd be caught.

The committee erupted in questions and comments. "Why were we told nothing of this?"

"Yes. They let us think the delay was because of the holiday weekend."

"We should have been told at once if our permits weren't valid!"

Through the balcony rail, I caught sight of Hoffman striding into the social hall. Goldsmith said, "Ah! Here's Herr Hoffman, the assistant manager of the HAPAG office. Perhaps he can tell us something."

"I'm sorry." Hoffman didn't look sorry. "I have no news for you."

"But," said Goldsmith, "when will these people be able to leave the ship?"

Hoffman shrugged. "It's all a matter for the proper authorities to decide."

"Who are these proper authorities?" said Josef Joseph, the head of the passenger committee. I knew him by sight.

"Ultimately, it is the President of Cuba who will decide." Hoffman spoke stiffly, without emotion.

Goldsmith spoke up to suggest a plan. "I'd like you, the committee members, to poll the passengers and come up with the names of friends and relatives in the U.S. Then the Joint will cable influential Americans to help."

"Good idea," a committee member said. "It might help to bring public pressure on the authorities."

"If they won't let you land in Cuba," Goldsmith said, "we'll work night and day to see that you're allowed to land somewhere else. There's no question of you returning to Germany."

Purser Mueller arrived in the social hall with a Cuban policeman. "Your visiting time on the ship is over," the policeman told Goldsmith and Hoffman. He led them away.

22

MS *St. Louis*, Havana Harbor
Monday, May 29

DAVID

THE CROWD OF PEOPLE watching the ship from the docks had grown in the afternoon, in spite of the heat. Small boats still surrounded the *St. Louis*, sellers of fruit and souvenirs as well as friends and family of passengers. And always the Cuban police boats circled the ship.

Passengers stood in nervous groups watching all the activity, whispering among themselves, fanning and wiping sweaty foreheads.

The day dragged on. Hannah had gone to her cabin again after we spied on the passenger committee meeting. I could tell she was having a hard time. Even though she didn't talk much about it, she was sad and worried about her parents in Germany and about whether we were going to be allowed to land.

I caught sight of Aaron Pozner who'd told me about being in a concentration camp. He was standing at the rail near the stern, where the red swastika flag drooped in the humidity. The last time I'd seen Pozner, he looked relaxed. Now his body was tense,

The Double Crossing

shoulders hunched with worry. Waiting in the heat, not knowing when we'd be allowed to land, was affecting all of us.

I was about to go down to talk to him, when a couple of crewmen walked up behind Pozner and spun him around roughly. I recognized the men as part of Schiendick's squad of Gestapo firemen. They took Pozner by the arms and hustled him across the deck toward the stairwell, where I couldn't see them.

I went to the stairwell where Pozner disappeared with the firemen, but there was no sign of them. Should I tell someone? I walked up and down the deck. After what seemed like a long time, while I was trying to decide who to tell, Pozner came back out of the stairwell. He paused in the doorway and looked around nervously. His clothes were rumpled. I hurried to him.

"What happened? I saw a couple of those Gestapo jerks take you away."

"*Diese Trottel!* The chumps! They said they had to search my cabin. Bullies see my shaved head and know I've been in a camp. That makes me a target. They locked the door and threw my things around. Smashed the picture of my family. When I tried to pick it up, they pushed me down on the floor. Tore up a letter from my wife, and my translation book. Told me it was time to shave my head again!"

"They can't do that! We should tell the captain! He'll stop them."

"No. No more trouble. We'll be off this ship soon and I'll never have to see *diese Schweine* again."

Before I could argue, Pozner pointed toward the accommodation ladder. "What's going on over there?"

A group of passengers, I counted thirteen, were climbing down toward the waiting ship's launch. The purser and several seamen and stewards stood watching from the top of the stairs.

"I recognize some of those passengers. They boarded the ship at Cherbourg," I said.

"Me too. I've talked to a couple of them. I think they're mostly Cubans and Spaniards. Looks like they get to go ashore. Thank God! Shouldn't be long for us."

I wanted to believe he was right. But after what I'd heard, I wondered whether the Jewish passengers would be going ashore at all. Without those thirteen, we now numbered 914.

"Listen, David, I don't want to talk to the captain about what happened. Right now I'm going to check on some of my friends who were in the camps, in case those Gestapo roughed them up too. Thanks."

"Okay, Aaron. I won't say anything."

Pozner walked away. I turned back to the rail to see the launch returning. Now a group of crewmen, including Otto Schiendick, had gathered at the top of the stairs, talking and laughing. As soon as the launch reached the mooring platform below, they climbed down the ladder and zoomed off in it toward shore.

This was it! Schiendick would have the chance to meet Hoffman and get the military secrets for Operation Sunshine!

I hurtled down the stairs to the lower decks two at a time, out of breath when I got to Hannah's cabin. She was there alone.

"Schiendick's gone ashore!" I blurted. "The launch took a group of crewmen. We've got to be watching when he comes back, to see if he brings anything on board."

"Come on! Leo probably knows when they're supposed to get back."

Hannah rushed out. I followed her as she hurried up three levels to the A deck, across it, and up to the bridge deck. Luckily, Leo was standing outside Captain Schroeder's day cabin.

When he saw us, he stepped forward, finger on his lips.

"Shh! He's meeting with his purser and first mate. He's in a terrible mood."

Keeping my voice low, I told Leo about seeing Schiendick leave. "Do you know when they're supposed to be back? In case he brings anything on board. Like the walking stick and magazines Hoffman had."

"I wish you could have gone with them," Hannah said. "You might have been able to stop him."

The Double Crossing

"Yeah. Maybe I could have caught up to him in a dark alley, shoved a knife in his back, taken the secret documents and destroyed them. Just my sort of thing."

I was surprised to hear Leo sound sarcastic. He'd always seemed pretty easy-going.

"That's not what I meant." Hannah sounded hurt. "I just thought ... I don't know."

"I'm sorry. Captain Schroeder has been in this monstrous, angry mood ever since Hoffman came this afternoon. Somehow, Hoffman made the captain order shore leave for the crew. And he said Schiendick had to be in the first boat. The captain practically spat out the order. He was furious. Usually he won't cave to anyone."

"Hoffman's probably a big deal in the *Abwehr*. He must be pretty powerful," I said.

"Yeah. Well, the shore leave ends at nine tonight. The launch will pick them up then, and they should get back pretty soon after that."

"Thanks, Leo," Hannah said. "I didn't mean ... I know you probably couldn't have done anything to stop him. But if he brings that stuff on board, we'll try to get rid of it."

"I wish you luck with that. Be careful."

• • •

After dinner Hannah and I went back on the deck and stood near the accommodation ladder. A little before nine, the launch left. It came back a half hour later with the crew members, including Schiendick.

Hannah poked me in the ribs. "Look! He's got them!"

Sure enough, by one of the ship's spotlights, we saw Schiendick get out of the boat carrying the walking stick and several magazines.

23

MS *St. Louis*, Havana Harbor
Tuesday, May 30

HANNAH

Last night we'd watched Schiendick come aboard with what had to be the secret military documents. Now we had to figure out how to destroy them to keep them out of Hitler's hands.

It was our fourth day in Havana Harbor and it dawned like a steam bath. I wasn't looking forward to living in this climate. If we even got off the ship, that is. I'd love to be sent home to Mother, but Germany wasn't safe for Jews. Everyone on the ship said so. It made me worry all the time about Mother and Father still being there.

At breakfast with David and his family, we talked about what the passenger committee was doing and what the captain was doing.

"Many passengers don't seem happy that Captain Schroeder stays on the bridge and doesn't talk to us," David's father said.

"He wants to help us." David came to the captain's defense. "He talks to the passenger committee. But he likes to have Purser Mueller and First Officer Ostermeyer answer passenger's questions."

"Well," his father continued, "we need to know what's going on. I hope the Joint will be able to get the Cuban government to accept us. That Benitez should be made to stand behind those landing permits he sold."

"Excuse me, Herr Jantzen," I said. "Can you explain about the Joint? I keep hearing they're trying to help us. Who are they?"

"The Joint is the American Jewish Joint Distribution Committee. They've been around a long time, since before the Great War. They raise funds, give legal support, and help Jews around the world. They're negotiating with the Cubans for us."

"I see. Do you think they'll have any luck?" I asked.

All our eyes went to Herr Jantzen. He cleared his throat. "Well, they've got a big organization with some money behind them. If anyone can get President Bru to let us land, they can."

• • •

After breakfast, David and I headed onto the deck. Already boats were circling the *St. Louis*. The crowd on the docks had grown. Some people carried signs. We couldn't tell if they were friends and family or people who didn't want us to land. We couldn't read the signs because David hadn't brought his binoculars. He was quieter than usual.

"David," I said, "we need a plan. How are we going to get those documents from Schiendick?"

"I don't know. How can we? We aren't cloak and dagger experts. We don't know anything about spy operations. We'll just get in trouble."

I was grouchy from the heat and the waiting. The talk and rumors made me tense. I exploded.

"We're going to stop him! Those are military secrets. We can't let Hitler get them." I wanted to scream. Didn't he understand how serious this was?

"Listen, Hannah. He probably has them in his room. Hidden. What can we do? Crew quarters are off limits to us." David gripped the railing, frowning. He looked as angry as I felt.

"Of course it won't be easy. But we can figure out a way, like when he's not in his cabin. Leo probably knows. Let's go talk to him." I turned to go.

"Now?" David trailed after me.

"Why not? Who knows how much time we have?"

On our way to the bridge deck, I saw a man from the passenger committee tacking carbon copies of telegrams on the bulletin board.

"What are these?" I asked.

"Captain Schroeder suggested the committee send telegrams to influential people, about our situation. It's a good idea. We're posting the carbons around the ship, to keep the passengers informed."

I read one addressed to the wife of the Cuban president.

OVER 900 PASSENGERS, 400 WOMEN AND CHILDREN, ASK YOU TO USE YOUR INFLUENCE AND HELP US OUT OF THIS TERRIBLE SITUATION. TRADITIONAL HUMANITARIANISM OF YOUR COUNTRY AND YOUR WOMAN'S FEELINGS GIVE US HOPE THAT YOU WILL NOT REFUSE OUR REQUEST.

If the telegrams worked, we might not have much time. We needed to find Leo and stop Schiendick before we got off the ship.

David followed me toward the bridge deck stairs. "Listen, Hannah. Wait a minute. I'm sorry. I don't want us to be mad at each other."

I stopped and faced him, my stomach churning. "I just … I feel like we have to do something. And it seems like you don't understand. Like you don't think it matters."

"I do. I know it matters. But I feel helpless." He reached out a hand, but let it drop.

"Like I said, let's find Leo. He can probably tell us where Schiendick's cabin is and maybe when he won't be there." I didn't want to argue with David. I wished he'd see how important this was.

When we got to the bridge deck, instead of running into Leo, we met Captain Schroeder stepping out of his cabin.

The Double Crossing

"Just who I wanted to see. Come in for a few minutes."

David and I exchanged a look and followed the captain inside. What was this about?

"Have a seat, please." He sat down at his desk and cleared his throat. "This conversation is strictly confidential. Can I count on you?"

"Yes, of course. Right, David?"

"Of course. I'm honored that you trust us."

"Good. I had a most unpleasant visit from Herr Hoffman, the assistant manager of the Cuban HAPAG office. I understand from Leo that you already have some knowledge of a certain situation."

Heart thumping, I nodded. So did David. Had Leo told the captain about Operation Sunshine?

"As you know, Otto Schiendick is the *Nationalsozialisten Ortsgruppenleiter* on board, in charge of keeping up Party standards and morale. And as I believe you also know, he has a group of Gestapo agents working with him. Hoffman told me that he, Hoffman, is the head of the *Abwehr* in Cuba. You know what that is?"

We both nodded again.

"I wasn't intending to give the crew shore leave until the passengers were allowed to go ashore. However, Hoffman ordered me to begin shore leave at once and to have Schiendick in the first group. So, against my wishes, I had to let Schiendick go ashore yesterday afternoon with some other crewmen." The captain paused and looked questioningly at us.

"We saw him," David said.

"I talked to Leo about this yesterday evening," the captain went on. "I asked him to keep an eye on Schiendick and let me know of any unusual activities. That's when he told me that you two had overheard something." He looked at us again. I felt his hazel eyes probing me.

"He told me you two heard him boast that he's an *Abwehr* courier and that he was planning to take stolen secret documents to Germany."

"That's right," David said. "He was talking to one of his Gestapo men. And we saw him bring the things Hoffman wanted to give him when he came back last night."

Leo had said Captain Schroeder was a loyal German, even if he wasn't a Nazi. But it seemed like he was on our side in this.

"He said it's called Operation Sunshine," I said. "Hoffman was supposed to give Schiendick information about the United States military. We think that's what he brought back. Thank goodness you know about it. We didn't know what to do. But you can stop him. Right?"

Captain Schroeder shook his head. "I wish it were that easy. I don't like my ship being used this way. It's no secret that I'm not fond of the Party. But to interfere would cost me my job, even my life, when I return to Germany. And I have a family."

My heart sank. "So, then, it's still up to me and David to stop him?" I looked at David. His eyes widened.

"Absolutely not," Captain Schroeder sounded suddenly stern, even angry. "First of all, you should have come to me with this information right away. And second, this is not something for you two youngsters to meddle in. As I'm sure you know, the *Abwehr* and the Gestapo are dangerous. Anyway," his voice softened, "I expect you'll be off the ship soon and it will be out of your hands."

I began to feel desperate again. Even the captain couldn't do anything? "But, if Hitler is planning to start a war, someone has to stop him from getting this information."

"That's not a job for you young people."

"Then who …?"

David put a hand on my arm and shook his head.

"C'mon. Let's go." He stood. "Thanks Captain Schroeder."

"I appreciate your confirming Schiendick's involvement," said the captain. "Remember, strictly confidential. And don't do anything dangerous."

As we were leaving the captain's cabin, the loud roar of an engine made us look up. A sea plane came to rest on the water on pontoon floats, not far from the *St. Louis*. The roar subsided to a rough idle.

Captain Schroeder came to the door to look. "That must be the lawyers from the Joint, coming to negotiate with the Cubans. Do you know about that?"

We both nodded.

"I pray to God they're successful!" said Captain Schroeder.

"So do we," I said.

"Thank you, sir," said David.

As we descended the stairway from the bridge deck, David whispered, "See? If even Captain Schroeder can't do anything, what can we do?"

"If the captain can't do anything, we have to. Whatever he says. Even if we get in trouble. Because we know about it. And it's wrong. It could mean war!"

24

MS *ST. LOUIS*, HAVANA HARBOR
TUESDAY, MAY 30

DAVID

SINCE OUR TALK with the captain and my argument with Hannah, I'd been going around and around in my head. If you know something is wrong, do you have to try to stop it? Even if you don't have much of a chance? Even if it's dangerous? And even if the grown-ups in charge tell you not to?

After lunch, I took my binoculars and walked the decks. My stomach churned. I'd been too upset to eat much. I looked through the binoculars at an unfamiliar gull. It was a Ring Billed Gull. I'd seen a picture in one of the captain's books on American birds.

My thoughts kept going back to Hannah and Operation Sunshine. Maybe all this thinking didn't matter. We might get off the ship tomorrow and not be able to do anything about Schiendick anyway. Wouldn't that be best? My head said "yes" it would. But my heart said Hannah was right. We should do whatever we could to stop the Nazi spy, if there was any chance.

The Double Crossing

As I was coming back around the port side on the A deck, I saw Hannah. My heart gave a little lurch. I'd missed her at lunch, though I'd seen her across the saloon eating with Ruth. Now her arms rested on the rail, chin in hands. A slight breeze lifted her hair in a rosy cloud. She was looking toward shore at the ever-growing crowd.

I hurried across the deck to stand next to her. I had to make things right between us, especially if we were leaving the ship soon.

"I'm sorry," I blurted. "I hope you aren't still mad at me. I've been thinking, and I guess you're right about stopping Schiendick. What do you think we should do?"

"I knew you'd understand! You're a good person, David. We can do it. I don't know how yet." Her green eyes searched mine.

Standing so close to her, I became uncomfortably conscious of my sweaty smell.

"Umm," I said, "I guess we could talk to Leo, since we can't ask the captain for help."

A door slammed, followed by the pounding of running footsteps. A passenger I recognized, a man about Papa's age, ran toward us across the deck. Horrified, I saw blood streaming from cuts on his wrists. I caught my breath. My heart almost stopped.

Hannah grabbed my hand, her nails digging in. A woman nearby shrieked. Before I could think or move to do anything, the man was at the rail. He climbed up and threw himself over, screamed as he fell and hit the water far below.

After a shocked moment, people rushed over, crowding us at the rail, yelling and crying out.

"Oh my God!" Hannah wailed. "Who is that? He's going to kill himself!"

I put an arm around her shoulder. We leaned out to look. The turquoise water was dark red where the man went under. I held my breath, as if it was me underwater.

At last the man popped to the surface. He began tearing at his arms, still streaming blood.

Sickened but fascinated, I couldn't take my eyes off him.

Crew members pushed past passengers racing across the decks to look down. A long blast came from the ship's horn. People screamed. Crewmen shouted orders. One of the police boats patrolling the ship made a sharp turn and sped toward the man in the water. Other boats headed that way.

Below us, on the B deck, a crewman climbed onto the rail. Another crewman appeared beside him yelling, "Meier! *Nein!*" The first crewman shook him off and dove. He disappeared under the water. All around us people gasped or screamed. Several heart-stopping seconds went by before he surfaced in the pool of blood next to the flailing passenger.

"*Mörder!* Nazi murderers! You'll never get me!" screamed the passenger.

Before the crewman, Meier, could grab him, the bleeding man dived underwater again. Meier went after him and, in a moment, pulled him up by the hair.

"Let me die!" the man shrieked and thrashed.

It looked like the seaman wouldn't be able to hold on. Then the police boat arrived beside them. A couple of policemen dragged the struggling passenger into the boat. A moment later they helped Meier climb on board. One of the policemen started to bandage the passenger's wrists.

With a burst of energy, the man kicked the policeman away and scrabbled toward the side of the boat yelling, "Let me die! Let me die!"

Meier tackled him again and the three of them dragged him back. The two policemen straddled the thrashing man, held him down and finished bandaging his wrists. The boat sped toward shore.

I felt light-headed. I'd never seen someone try to kill himself. And in such a gruesome way.

"Oh, my God," Hannah said. "That was horrible. Who was that?"

"I don't know his name. I've seen him, though. He's Fritz's father. You know, that boy who just had his thirteenth birthday?"

"Max Loewe," said my father, behind us.

I took my arm from Hannah's shoulder and turned around. "I didn't know you were there."

Papa's skin was pale, his eyes wide. The only other time I'd seen him look so upset was after his dental office was destroyed on *Kristallnacht*.

"I heard the man overboard signal, that long blast on the horn. I just got here. But everyone's saying it's Max Loewe. He was a lawyer in Breslau. Before. A decorated Great War veteran. Nerves shattered by the Nazis, I heard." He looked down, shaking his head. "What a tragedy!"

The boat arrived at the dock. A loud bell clanged. Policemen pushed back the huge crowd, making a path for the arriving ambulance. Attendants lifted Herr Loewe onto a stretcher and loaded him in the back of the ambulance. A couple of policemen helped Meier get in and climbed in after him.

"If you two are all right, I'm going to check on your mother and Rebekah," Papa said.

"Okay, Papa." As he turned away, I raised my binoculars again to focus on the shore. Men with notebooks and cameras had made their way through the crowd. They were talking to police and taking pictures. Reporters. Like buzzards circling.

The attendants closed the doors and the ambulance slowly made its way through the crowd. It rushed away, lights flashing, bells clanging and fading in the distance.

The ship was in an uproar. People milled around. Others stood in groups, talking and crying. I held onto Hannah's hand. I'd never seen so many grown-ups crying as in the last few days.

"The Nazis tortured him in one of the camps," someone said.

"It was the last straw, the fear of being sent back to Germany."

"Are you all right?" I asked Hannah.

"Not really." She was pale, beads of sweat on her forehead. I led her to a deck chair and sat down beside her.

Somehow reporters were on the ship, going around with pads and pencils, talking to passengers. One of them, a skinny young Cuban with a thick accent, approached us and asked, "You see anything, kid?"

I was about to tell him to leave us alone, when one of the ship's officers arrived.

"You have to leave the ship right now. I don't know how any of you got on board. No one's allowed." He took the reporter by the arm and led him away, past a crewman scrubbing blood off the deck.

Hannah's face was still pale. Her cold hands shook. After a while, when things quieted down, she stood up.

"I need to change before dinner."

"Okay." I stood too. "Maybe you should lie down for a little while. Do you need help?"

Her eyes filled with tears. She leaned into me for a moment and I awkwardly patted her back. "I'll be all right," she said. "It's … it made me think about my father. Don't worry. See you at dinner."

Before I could think what to say, she turned and hurried across the deck. I wished I could have done something to make her feel better. She's all alone. Her father's in a camp.

The vision of Herr Loewe running, bleeding, and jumping kept flashing through my mind. The numbers popped into my head: 913 passengers now, if he doesn't come back.

• • •

At dinner Hannah's eyes were red. She didn't look like she'd rested.

We tried to be careful what we said about Herr Loewe in front of Rebekah, but she'd already heard lurid stories from the other kids.

The Double Crossing

"Heinrich Meier, the brave crewman who jumped in to rescue him, came back a little while ago," Papa said. "Loewe is probably going be in the hospital for a while."

"Are they going to let his wife and children go ashore to be with him?" Mama asked.

"No. The Cuban policeman in charge on the ship asked the government officials. They said no passengers will be allowed on shore under any circumstances."

"That's barbaric!" Mama said. "If they turn us back, he and his family will be separated."

Rebekah looked at our mother with alarm. She turned to Papa. "They aren't going to send us back, are they, Papa?"

"Don't worry, Liebling. Everyone's doing everything possible to get us to safety."

After dinner, I walked back outside with Hannah. I wanted to find a dark, quiet corner to say goodnight. She seemed so sad. But there was no such place. The number of police boats circling the *St. Louis* had at least doubled. Lifeboats had been lowered to the decks. Sailors stood by them, ready for another rescue if needed. Lights dangled over the sides of the ship, illuminating the glassy surface of the water, a dark shroud surrounding us.

It felt like a prison ship.

25

MS *St. Louis*, Havana Harbor
Wednesday, May 31

Hannah

Every time I closed my eyes, I saw Herr Loewe running across the deck, streaming blood from his wrists, and jumping over the side. I turned restlessly from side to side, trying to keep my eyes open.

Was Father being tortured like Herr Loewe was? Was Mother all right?

Morning finally came. As I made my way to breakfast, I still felt distracted and uneasy. My eyes were like sandpaper. The deck already shimmered with heat. In the dining saloon, people sat glumly quiet or talked in low voices. I sat at the Jantzen's table, but none of us felt like making conversation.

After breakfast David and I sat in deck chairs in the shade, talking and fanning ourselves with folded newspapers.

"Have you been hearing that we're going to be sent back to Germany?" I said. "To concentration camps? Like my father."

The Double Crossing

"Yes. I've heard that. Mama and Papa try to act normal, but I can see how tense they are."

"Ruth heard there might be a suicide pact among the passengers, if we head back. People would throw themselves off the ship." Herr Loewe's scream rang in my head again.

David grimaced.

"Ruth told me not to worry, she wouldn't do it. But a lot of passengers would do anything to stay out of the camps. I'm scared. But there's one good thing about still being on the ship," I said.

"You mean that we still get to be together?" He smiled.

I smiled back. "Okay. Two good things. We still have a chance to stop Operation Sunshine. Yesterday, after what happened, I almost forgot about it. But we need to do something. Today."

"Like what?"

"Get into Schiendick's room and find the walking stick and magazines. And get rid of them." A terrifying idea, but the only way I could think to stop him.

David frowned. He clasped his hands in his lap, staring at nothing.

I fidgeted until, feeling impatient, I said, "Well?"

"I'm thinking."

His blond hair clung to his head, damp with sweat. He stared down in concentration. "All I can think of are reasons why we shouldn't do that. Number one is that Captain Schroeder said not to interfere."

I clenched my fists. "But yesterday you said you were in. Sometimes you have to do what's right! No matter what people tell you."

"Okay, here are the problems." He held up one finger. "We don't know where Schiendick's room is, except that it's probably in that 'Crew Only' area." He held up the next finger. "Even if we did know, the room's probably locked." He held up a third finger. "And if we did get rid of them, Schiendick would notice. He'd go after whoever did it." He closed his hand.

144

"If we did do it," he went on, "the trick would be to find the papers, or microfilm, or whatever's hidden in those things and get rid of that. We should leave the walking stick and magazines. He might not notice. At least not right away."

"That's really smart. So we just have to figure out where his cabin is, how to get in, and when he won't be there."

"Do you hear yourself? We can't do any of that. What about telling the passenger committee?"

"The passenger committee? What could they do?" Now I felt frustrated with him all over again. "They don't have any power. Not like Schiendick and those Gestapo guys."

"Exactly! And what power do we have?"

We were still arguing when Leo showed up.

"Hi, you two. Have you heard? The *St. Louis* is all over the news today."

"What news?" I asked. "What does it say?"

"The New York Times for one. They had a big article about the passenger who tried to commit suicide. And about how Cuba hasn't let you go ashore. A lot of the papers in the U.S. had articles, mostly saying Cuba should let you land."

He sighed and sat down in the next deck chair, wiping his forehead. "I can't believe how hot it is." Lowering his voice, he said, "Unfortunately, there's been a lot in the German news too. Propaganda from Goebbels. They're saying the situation with Cuba shows no one wants the Jews. The captain thinks that was the Nazi's plan in the first place, to let you leave and then stir things up against you. That way they can say they aren't the only ones who don't like Jews."

I felt tears pressing behind my eyes. The Nazi's were purely evil to come up with a plan like that. All the more reason to stop them from getting American secrets.

"Leo," I said, "we were just talking about how to get rid of that information Schiendick is smuggling. He has the walking stick now. We need your help. Do you know where his room is and—"

"I don't know if we should do it," David interrupted. "The captain knows, and he told us not to."

Leo looked from me to David. "I sort of agree with both of you. It doesn't seem right not to do anything. But if Schiendick and his Gestapo caught you or found out you did it—" He swiped a finger across his neck.

We needed his help.

"Leo, please—"

He frowned. "I shouldn't get involved… but I'd love to stop Schiendick's scheme. I bet the Party wouldn't be so happy with him then. I can help with some things, like telling you where his room is. But you have to be careful. It's not just him. He has a roommate, Heinrich, one of his Gestapo gang."

"The one we heard him talking to about Operation Sunshine!" I said.

"I think I can get you a key to their cabin from the purser's office. And I'll find out what shifts Schiendick and the other guy are working. That's about all I can do."

"That's enough." I looked at David. "We can do the rest. Right?"

David looked down, biting his lip. He cleared his throat. "Umm—"

"Sorry, I've got to go," said Leo. "I'll find you after lunch." He stood and walked quickly across the deck.

"We should do it this afternoon. While we have a chance. In case we do get off the ship," I said.

David sat frowning. He didn't say anything.

I couldn't tell what he was thinking. He'd have to make up his own mind. Right now, I didn't feel like arguing. And he didn't look like he was ready to make plans. I'd do it by myself if he wouldn't help. I stood up.

"I'm going to the library. Maybe there's a book that I haven't read yet. See you at lunch?"

"Yeah. See you then."

After lunch, Leo caught up to us on the promenade deck. "*Mannomann!* I've never seen the captain in such a mood. He's worried about more suicides or even," he whispered, "mutiny." He looked around and went on in a low voice. "He just met with a representative of the Cuban president. The captain gave him a letter to take back to President Bru. But he doesn't have a lot of hope."

A weight dragged me down. I didn't have a lot of hope either.

"Also, the captain has asked the passenger committee to pick some level-headed men to do patrols every night. They'll take shifts and walk the decks, to prevent more suicides.

"I have some good news, though, about your plan. I got you a key to Schiendick's cabin." He held out a room key. "Just be sure to give it back when you're done. I don't think the purser will miss it soon. He has so many keys."

Before David could move to take the key, I reached for it and slipped it into my pocket. "Thanks, Leo. You're amazing."

Leo went on, speaking quietly, "The bad news is that Schiendick and his roommate are on opposite shifts, so one of them could be in the room any time. That's the schedule tomorrow and Friday too. You might be able to get in and out while they're at dinner, but it could be risky. They only have a half hour, right before the passengers eat. Their cabin is in the crew quarters, aft on the D deck. The third cabin on the left after you go through the door that says, 'Crew Only.'" He turned to leave, then turned back. "Whatever you do, don't get caught, for my sake and yours."

After Leo left, David stared out at the water, then dropped his head down onto his hands on the railing.

"What is it, David?" I asked. I put my hand on his back.

"The Cubans aren't going to let us off the ship, are they?"

It took a moment for me to find my voice. "It doesn't look like it." I hesitated. "Okay. Things seem bad. But remember, Captain Schroeder said he'll take us to the United States, if we

The Double Crossing

can't land here. And ... we have the key to Schiendick's cabin." I tried to smile but couldn't quite manage it.

David sighed. "Yeah. We have that. Sounds like we have time, too. I mean, if we aren't getting off the ship today, we can wait. We need to make a good plan—not rush into it. In fact, if we can't get off the ship, we may have a lot of time."

"Ooh!" I groaned.

David put an arm around my shoulder. "It'll be all right."

I let the tears come. It was all too horrible, being unwanted in Cuba, not knowing where I'd end up, or how Mother and Father would get to me. Thank goodness, I had David as a friend. I got my tears under control and dug out a handkerchief to blow my nose.

"Tomorrow, okay?" I said. "We can make a plan in the morning and do it when they go to dinner."

26

MS *St. Louis*, Havana Harbor
Thursday, June 1, 1939

DAVID

"C'MON! HURRY UP!" Rebekah was up and ready to go to breakfast before I dragged myself out of bed. Mama had told my sister to enjoy her final time on the ship and she'd taken it to heart.

"It's a perfect day for swimming after breakfast." She peered out the porthole. "See how blue the sky is? It's going to be great living here!"

"Okay. I'm coming. You go ahead."

I almost always have a good appetite, but this morning my stomach was uneasy. All I could think about was suicides, mutiny, concentration camps, and, on top of it all, sneaking into Otto Schiendick's cabin to steal military documents meant for the *Abwehr*.

Hannah was determined to do it today. It gave me chills to think of it. But I couldn't let her do it alone. And, like she said, it was the right thing to do.

The Double Crossing

Hannah wasn't at breakfast. Maybe she didn't have an appetite either. I went up to the B deck to watch for her. The usual sights in the harbor, the boats around the ship, the people on shore, became a blur as I tried to work out the details of a plan. We'd have to be fast. Should one of us stand watch? Outside the "Crew Only" door or outside Schiendick's cabin? But a lookout hanging around where they weren't supposed to be might get noticed.

Some younger children clustered around one of the Cuban policemen. The kids had made friends with all of them. Rebekah wasn't with the group. She'd be in the pool by now. One boy was wearing the officer's hat. A girl asked, "*Que hora es?* What time is it?"

The officer replied that it was a little past "*diez hora*," ten o'clock.

The girl, using her new Spanish words, asked when we would be able to go to Havana, "*A qué hora ir a Havana?*"

The children and the policeman all answered together like a chorus, "*mañana.*" Everyone laughed. Mañana, tomorrow, was what the policemen always said.

Hannah appeared, looking as tense as I felt. "What's funny?" she asked, nodding at the children. I told her.

"Well, at least the kids are having fun." She put a hand on my arm. "We're doing it tonight, right? When Schiendick and his cabin mate are at dinner. Every day we wait means we could lose our chance."

I would rather have done almost anything else, but seeing her anxious face, her intense green eyes, I agreed.

"Yes," I said. "I've been trying to come up with a plan. All I've got is, I think we should stick together. If anyone sees us, we'll say we got lost."

"I'm scared," she said.

I took her warm, moist hands. "Me too."

"Really?" she said. "You look so calm."

• • •

I was keeping an eye out for Leo, but it wasn't until after lunch when I caught sight of him coming down the stairs from the bridge deck. He looked upset and distracted.

"What's going on?" I asked.

Leo took hold of my arm and led me back into a corner by the lifeboats.

"The captain heard, unofficially from a news report, that we're going to be ordered to leave the harbor. He's gone ashore to talk to the Cuban president and straighten things out."

Leave the harbor? I thought of Pozner's concentration camp stories. Is that where we'd end up?

Leo put a hand on my shoulder. "Don't worry. The captain will reason with the Cubans. He said he should have gone ashore a long time ago and dealt with things himself, not left it to politicians and lawyers."

I was only a little reassured. Making sure no one was in ear shot, I lowered my voice to a whisper. "Just so you know—we decided to go ahead this evening. We're going to get that stuff from Shiendick's cabin."

"You'll have to work fast. I know I've said this before but be careful. You don't want to tangle with Schiendick and his Gestapo bullies."

"You're right about that."

"The ship can't leave tonight. Even if the Cubans order us to. It takes hours for the engines to warm up. And we have to take on food and water." Leo sounded calm, but the worried crease between his eyebrows gave him away.

• • •

Later that afternoon, Hannah and I watched the activity around the ship and on the dock. A man in a boat brought a couple of pineapples and had them passed up to his wife and children on the *St. Louis*.

The Double Crossing

"It's sad," I said. "The families are so close, waiting on shore, while their loved ones are trapped on this ship."

"I know."

A low rumble vibrated under our feet. Everyone on the deck jerked to attention. Hannah grabbed my arm. "What's that?"

Someone yelled, "It's the engines! They've started the engines!"

A group of women passengers who were gathered near the accommodation ladder began screaming.

"We have to get off!"

The women pushed forward, rushing toward the ladder, trying to get off the ship. Three policemen stationed there pushed back and were nearly overcome. A pregnant woman, knocked back against the rail, collapsed.

"*Alto!* Halt!" The policemen drew their guns.

Other passengers joined the women and a panicked crowd formed. Hannah started forward toward the group, but I put a hand on her arm to stop her.

More police officers swarmed up the ladder from their boats. People yelled and screamed. The officers backed up against the rail, guns drawn, shouting back.

"Can't we do something?" Hannah said, taking another step forward.

"Stay back. They might shoot." I held onto her arm.

The engine noise vibrated the deck. The ship's boat arrived and docked at the platform. A man got out and hurried up the ladder. It took a moment for me to recognize the captain out of uniform. He wore an ordinary suit and hat.

Captain Schroeder looked shocked to walk into the middle of the screaming near-riot. First Officer Ostermeyer and Purser Mueller had arrived and stood between the police and the passengers, trying to calm everyone down.

The captain ordered the policemen to holster their weapons. At first, they didn't obey. Captain Schroeder yelled at them, and no one could doubt his authority. The police put away their guns.

"I'm sorry this happened," the captain said to the group of passengers. "However, nothing will be gained by this sort of demonstration. Please disperse now. Go back to your cabins or other activities."

"Is it true the ship is about to sail?" shouted a man from the crowd.

"Please be patient. The passenger committee is the correct channel for information. The committee will inform you of any sailing date." He sounded calm.

People grumbled, but the crowd started to break up. The passengers moved off to go below or stand along the railings, talking in low voices.

"That could have been bad, if he hadn't come," Hannah said. "What's going to happen? Why are the engines running?"

"We'll find out after the captain meets with the passenger committee. It doesn't look good."

"Well, whether we're going ashore or not, we have to go ahead with our plan." Hannah's face looked more determined than ever.

I sighed. "I know. Tonight. 6:30. Meet you in front of your cabin."

• • •

A couple of hours later, on my way to my cabin, I noticed a commotion around the bulletin board. A man from the passenger committee was posting a notice. I worked my way into the crowd of passengers and read:

> The Cuban government has ordered us to leave the harbor. We shall depart at 10:00 a.m. Friday morning. But our departure does not mean discussions with the Cuban government are ended. Only by leaving Havana can Mr. Berenson and his colleagues continue working. The ship will continue to be in contact with all Jewish organizations and other official bodies. They will all continue to try to arrange a landing outside Germany. In the meantime, the ship will remain close to the American coast.

The Double Crossing

My head pounded. Passengers crowded around the notice.
"That's not right! They can't make us leave!"
A woman screamed and sobbed. She was about to fall to the deck when someone caught her and led her away. Several other people began crying.

It was frightening to see the adults panic. I didn't believe the notice told us the real situation. Berenson was the lawyer from the Joint who was talking with the Cuban government. But if there was still a chance the Cubans were going to let us land, why send us away?

27

MS *St. Louis*, Havana Harbor
Thursday, June 1, 1939

HANNAH

"I'M DOING IT NOW. Like we said." It was an effort to keep my voice down.

"I just meant we should wait. We're not going to get off the ship right away. If we're still on board, and Schiendick figures out it was us ... well, more chance of getting caught."

"If I put it off any longer, I might lose my nerve," I said.

We'd met up in the corridor in front of my cabin like we planned. The engines throbbed louder down here, adding to my tension. I was ready to go, and I'd expected David would be too.

Whether we finally landed in Cuba, the United States, or Germany, preventing Operation Sunshine was a way to fight back against Hitler and his Nazis. They'd taken my home and destroyed my family. I was going to do what I could to stop them.

"Okay. We'll do it now." David was pale, the black centers of his eyes almost swallowing the blue.

"Come on." I started up the corridor and David followed.

The Double Crossing

We walked aft to a closed door with a sign: NO PASSENGERS BEYOND THIS POINT. No one was in sight. Heart racing, I turned the handle of the door and pushed it open. On the other side, the passage continued empty and much the same as the passenger corridor, lined with cabin doors.

When we reached the third door on the left, David tried the knob. Of course, it was locked. I passed him the key. Fumbling, he almost dropped it. When he tried to put it into the keyhole, his hands shook so much he couldn't make it fit.

"Here, let me try."

He gave me back the key. I managed to steady my hand enough to get the key into the hole and turn it.

"Okay." I pushed the door open a crack and stuck my head in. My heart pounded in my throat. The room was empty, but there was a warmth or a sensation that made me feel someone had just left.

I crept inside, David on my heels. He closed the door silently behind him. I let out the breath I was holding. The smells of cigarette smoke and men's sweat made me wrinkle my nose.

The room was even smaller than mine in tourist class. The beds were neatly made. A small portrait of Hitler hung on the wall over one bunk.

"There." I pointed. The walking stick Schiendick had brought on board leaned in a corner.

David whispered back, "And the magazines."

A small stack of magazines sat on the bedside table.

"Why would he leave it all out like that?" I crossed the small space to the bunk and picked up the walking stick. "It must come apart."

"Let me see," David mouthed.

I handed it to him and began flipping through the magazines.

Nothing! I'd expected to find something hidden between the pages. Papers. Photographs. Microfilm. I felt discouraged.

David held the two halves of the walking stick. He'd pulled it apart. It was hollow inside. Empty.

"No wonder he left them out. He must have hidden everything. Must be here somewhere." I opened the drawer of the bedside table. It held only a copy of Hitler's book, *Mein Kampf*, a folded handkerchief, and a bottle of pills. I riffled the book's pages, finding nothing.

David finished searching the narrow dresser. He shook his head and moved on to the wardrobe. I squeezed behind him on my way to the bathroom, catching a glimpse of stewards' uniforms in the wardrobe.

We had to hurry! My hands shook as I opened the door of the miniscule bathroom. One glance told me nothing could possibly be hidden there.

"Hannah!" David held a steel box, about the size of a shoe box. "It was under his bed. It's locked."

I crossed the room in three steps and reached for the box. It had no latch other than the keyhole. The lid wouldn't open. When I shook it, I could hear the shuffling of papers inside. "This has to be it. What shall we do? If we take it, he'll know right away."

Footsteps sounded in the corridor outside, coming closer. We both froze. I got a sick feeling in my stomach. David's face drained of color.

Keys jingled outside the door. I seized David's arm. Our eyes locked. Where could we go? There was nowhere to hide.

"Hey, Otto!" a familiar voice called.

"It's Leo," David mouthed.

"What do you want?" Schiendick's unfriendly voice came from the other side of the door.

"Come talk to me on the deck a minute, where it's private. We've had some important news." Leo's voice was pitched louder than necessary.

The footsteps thumped away.

"Leo's giving us a chance to get away," whispered David. "But we can't take the box. Schiendick will know Leo was involved."

The Double Crossing

"You're right. Put everything back like it was." Trembling, I closed the bathroom door and straightened the magazines.

David slid the metal box under the bunk. He tried to push the ends of the walking stick back together, fumbling, about to drop one of the pieces.

I jumped to grab it, knocking a magazine off the table. David caught the end of the cane. The magazine hit the floor with a slap that sounded like a shot.

I held my breath, listening. I didn't hear anyone.

David put the walking stick together and set it in its place.

Picking up the magazine, I set it on top of the others and nodded toward the door.

We tiptoed across the room. David opened the door a crack, looked out and gestured for me to follow.

I followed him out, closing the door silently, and checked it was locked. We hurried back to the door into the passenger area. David reached for the handle.

He jumped back when the door opened toward him. A crewman nearly slammed into him. With horror, I recognized one of Schiendick's Gestapo firemen. He looked confused, then angry. I was sure he must hear the mad thumping of my heart.

"What are you doing here? This area's off limits to passengers!" He was red in the face. A vein pulsed at his temple.

David seemed unable to speak. "We ... we ..."

"We're sorry." My voice came out as a squeak. "We came the wrong way. We were just going back."

"Can't you *dumm Juden* read? No passengers allowed!"

"Yes, sir. It was a mistake," David croaked.

"I better not catch you here again!" The fuming seaman practically shoved us out the door and closed it forcefully behind us.

I seethed inside. Another Nazi bully pushing me around. As soon as we were well away from the restricted area, I said, "Now what are we going to do?"

"C'mon. We'll figure it out." He held out his hand and I gripped it anxiously. It was as slick with sweat as mine. "Let's go up on the deck."

• • •

The sun, a glowing orange ball, hung low over the water. My head pounded. I couldn't think what to do next. We'd come so close. We had the papers in our hands!

It took me a few moments to notice the change in the scene on the deck. Passengers leaned over the rails, many sobbing openly. I peered over the side. Dozens of boats swarmed around the ship, filled with family members of passengers, waving and calling good-byes. A few held out their arms, as if begging their loved ones to jump the five stories to the water. Men and women alike were crying. So were their relatives on the ship. People moaned and cried out.

Underneath all the crying and wailing, the pounding of the engines increased. The setting sun painted the harbor crimson and a brilliant full moon rose, hovering like a ghost over the *St. Louis*.

28

MS *St. Louis*, Havana Harbor
Friday, June 2, 1939

DAVID

I DREAMED I was being chased through the bowels of the ship by Gestapo agents. Someone was crying. I opened my eyes to see Rebekah sitting on the side of her bed, sobbing.

"Bekah, what's wrong?"

"I'm afraid. Are we going back to Germany?"

"No. No."

I got out of bed. The ship wasn't moving yet. We must not have left the harbor. I sat beside Rebekah and put an arm around her shoulder.

"Captain Schroeder won't let them send us back. He'll take us somewhere safe. Come on. Let's get dressed and go find Mama."

After breakfast, I went on the deck to face another sweltering day. The vibration of the engines was a constant reminder that we would soon leave the harbor. The water was empty of the small boats that had brought relatives and Cuban vendors. Several

The Double Crossing

police launches surrounded the ship, keeping other boats from approaching.

The scene on shore was out of control. A solid mass of people filled the dock area and nearby streets. What must have been tens of thousands of people watched the *St. Louis*. The distant roar of voices, chanting, and yelling carried to the ship. The occasional words I picked out were in Spanish, but the crowd didn't sound friendly.

I kept thinking about our close call in Schiendick's room. What had Leo said to Schiendick when he called him away?

Stationing myself near the bridge deck stairs, I watched for Leo.

"I don't have much time," he said when he came down the stairs. "We're getting ready to sail." We walked along the promenade together, talking quietly.

"Thanks for yesterday. You saved our skins."

"Good thing I decided to play look-out. You didn't take the documents, did you?" He gave me an anxious look.

"We found them. Or we think so. In a locked metal box. But we didn't take it. He'd have suspected you were involved."

"Thank goodness. I've been worried. You're right, he would have suspected me."

"What did you tell him?" I asked.

"Just that we'd received orders from the Cuban government to leave the harbor so talks could continue. Probably nothing he didn't know." Leo frowned, rubbing the back of his neck nervously.

"What did he say?"

"He was angry. He said we had to get back to Germany. He had important things to do. He acted like it was my fault we weren't going straight back. He said, 'I'm reporting the captain and Purser Mueller to the Party for their behavior on this trip. And I'm asking the Party to investigate you, Jockl. I suspect you might be a Jew yourself!' He gave me such a hateful look."

"What? Why would he think that?"

Leo hesitated. "My mother was Jewish. I wasn't brought up Jewish, but technically I am. Don't tell anyone. I don't know how he suspected. Only Captain Schroeder knows."

"Gosh! Can I just tell Hannah? We won't tell anyone else."

Leo hesitated only a heartbeat. "Of course. You two are a set, like salt and pepper shakers." He laughed and I smiled, liking that idea.

"You'd better not be involved with us in the spy thing anymore," I said. "Too risky."

"You're a good friend, David. I trust you. Don't worry. The captain won't take you back to Germany. Got to go. We'll talk later."

• • •

I walked around, tense and fidgety, unable to settle. Aaron Pozner was standing by the rail, staring blankly at the water. Tears streamed down his face. I crossed the deck and joined him.

"I haven't cried since I said good-bye to my wife and children," Pozner rubbed his eyes. "I'd begun to hope. And now … I tell you what. I won't go back to Germany. I'll do whatever's necessary. They're never getting me into one of those camps again!"

Before I could answer, a chant started, voices repeating, "We must not sail. We must not die. We must not sail …" Over and over.

Pozner raised his eyebrows. "Sounds like it's coming from the social hall. There's supposed to be a meeting."

"Let's go," I said.

An unruly scene met us. Over a hundred passengers, mostly men, were inside, chanting. The members of the passenger committee were trying to call people to order. I saw Papa, and we pushed through the crowd to join him.

A couple of men burst into the hall. "A police launch just arrived! Six passengers were escorted down by Cuban police, and the launch took them to the dock. They let them go!"

Word spread through the crowd and the chanting stopped.

"What?"

"Why them?"

The Double Crossing

"What about the rest of us?"

People began rushing toward the doors.

The head of the committee, Herr Joseph, banged on the table, shouting for order. "We'll go and ask Purser Mueller, or the captain. If they let some of us land, maybe there's hope for others."

The passenger committee hurriedly filed out and the room continued to buzz with angry talk. Some people left. Others stayed to wait for the committee members to return.

"I'm going to talk to my friends," Pozner said. "I want to know the mood, and what they're willing to do in case we head back to Germany."

Papa stared after him. "I have a feeling Herr Pozner could stir up some trouble." He paused. "Maybe that's what we need at this point."

I waited with Papa for a while. When nothing more happened, I went back on the deck. Soon Hannah joined me.

"Oh, David! Everything's going wrong. We haven't stopped Schiendick. They won't let us into Cuba. And the mail just came, with nothing from my mother." She covered her face, sobbing.

I reached my arms around her and patted her back. I didn't know how to comfort her. There was nothing I could say.

The loudspeaker crackled with an announcement. "The passenger committee will address all the passengers in the social hall."

Hannah straightened up, hiccoughing, and swiped at her eyes. I brushed a tear off her cheek.

"Let's go," she said.

I was relieved to hear her sound more like herself.

Men, women, and even children packed into the social hall, filling the entire space, many of them crying. Hannah and I squeezed in at the back just as the passenger committee was filing onto the platform, looking grim. They were followed by two men I recognized: Robert Hoffman, the spy master from HAPAG, and Milton Goldsmith from the Jewish Relief Committee. A Cuban police officer and a couple of other men crowded in behind them.

Goldsmith and the Cubans appeared serious, Hoffman stern and unsympathetic.

Goldsmith wiped sweat from his forehead with a handkerchief and cleared his throat. "Sisters and brothers, do not give up hope. Be strong." He looked apologetic and miserable, not strong at all.

He went on to say that the Joint committee and many important people would work so that we could land outside Germany, and that the passenger committee would receive frequent reports from relief organizations in the United States.

Unhappy silence filled the hall.

The Cuban police officer stepped forward, twisting his hat in his hand. "I am very sorry," he said. "We have to do our duty as police officers, but we wish from our hearts, that you will land soon."

Hoffman didn't say anything. He led the group off the platform without even a glance at the passengers.

By the time we arrived on deck, Hoffman was already in the launch. The other men followed down the accommodation ladder, including all the Cuban police officers stationed on the ship.

While the HAPAG launch sped back to shore, the *St. Louis'* engines revved louder. The horn blasted and the ship began to move out of the harbor. I made another count in my head. Thirty passengers had left the ship, one way or another, including Herr Weiler, the man who died at sea, and Herr Loewe, who tried to commit suicide. And the two little girls and the others who'd been allowed to go ashore. That left 907 passengers still on board. No one seemed to know why those six passengers were allowed to leave today.

Some of the passengers waved to the crowds on shore. Others cried. Most watched in silence. Crew members patrolled behind the passengers, watching us closely. A couple of times a crewman jumped to grab a passenger who leaned too far over the rail.

"They're afraid someone will jump." Hannah whispered, leaning close.

"Some people might. They'd have a chance to swim to shore."

The Double Crossing

Over twenty police launches escorted the *St. Louis* out of the harbor. Other small boats followed, carrying reporters, some filming with movie cameras. They shouted out questions.

"Where is the *St. Louis* headed now?"

"Will you go back to Germany?"

No one answered.

I held tight to Hannah's hand. The ship passed through the narrow entrance to the harbor, guarded by the ancient fortress with its castle. The spire pointed like a threatening finger lifted in warning. You shall not pass.

"They invited us. Now they're turning us out," said Hannah. "Doesn't anyone want us?"

I took a breath to say something. But what could I say?

PART THREE

29

MS *St. Louis*, Caribbean
Saturday, June 3, 1939

HANNAH

The rocking motion of the ship was a constant reminder that the *St. Louis* had left the harbor. We were cruising in the Caribbean, north of Cuba somewhere, and seemed to be traveling in circles going nowhere, like the movie in my head, my *kopfkino*.

While the ship waited in the harbor, Ruth had spent the evenings at a movie or dance with friends and slept late. Today, though, she was up early. "There's Shabbat service this morning. Let's get to breakfast."

I watched her comb her hair and put on lipstick in front of the small mirror in our miniature bathroom.

"How can you go on like everything's fine? We're in such a mess!" I said.

She closed the cap on the lipstick tube and blotted her lips with a piece of toilet paper.

The Double Crossing

"It's going to work out. Remember, you told me the captain would take us to the United States if Cuba won't let us in. You worry too much. We're on a luxury cruise. Have fun!"

"I did tell you that. But I'm not sure it's up to the captain."

"It'll be fine. You'll see." Ruth smiled. "And, guess what! I got a letter from my mother yesterday, before we left Havana. Oh! My gosh! I forgot to tell you. She said your mother had been sick but is feeling much better and will write soon. And there's no news of your father yet."

"What?" I glared at Ruth. "Why didn't you tell me yesterday? You know I've been dying to hear from her."

"I'm sorry. I hardly saw you. And with so much going on, I forgot. Anyway, it's old news now. My mother wrote it a few days after we left."

I tried to control my anger. Of course, the letter was old news. But how would Mother's letters reach me now that we'd left Cuba? Had people in Oldenburg heard that the *St. Louis* was turned away? Of course they had. It was just the sort of anti-Jewish propaganda the Nazis liked to spread. And Mother was probably worried about me.

• • •

The singing, Torah reading, and familiar rituals of Shabbat service lifted my spirits. When I parted from Ruth after the service, I said, "Sorry I was so gloomy. I feel better. I'll try to take your advice and have fun."

"That's my girl." Ruth grinned. "Worry won't solve anything."

The fresh ocean breeze on the deck felt marvelous after the heat of Havana. But in spite of what I'd told Ruth, worries crowded in again like flies buzzing around my head.

I wasn't the only uneasy passenger. As I walked around, looking for David, I overheard several anxious conversations. People doubted that negotiations with Cuba would be successful, now that we'd been made to leave. Everyone's worst fear was to be sent back to Germany.

I found David in our old meeting place, next to Peter's lifeboat, deep in conversation with Leo.

"Hi Hannah." Leo said. "Sorry you couldn't get rid of those documents. I wish I could do something to stop Schiendick, but he's already out to get me."

"You did what you could. You saved us. We don't want you to risk getting involved any more. But I'm not giving up."

David raised his eyebrows, questioning.

I shook my head. I didn't want to remind Leo I still had the key to Schiendick's room. I'd try again to get those documents. The key wouldn't be missed, with everything that was going on.

"I was telling David that Berenson, the lawyer from the refugee organization, still thinks he can get you into Cuba. He's negotiating with President Bru," said Leo.

"I don't trust the Cubans. They don't want us," I said.

"Well," Leo said, "There may be alternatives. The captain got a telegram from HAPAG in Germany. It said the Dominican Republic was willing to take you."

"The Dominican Republic?" asked David. "Isn't that another island close to Cuba? I saw it on the map in the social hall."

"Yes. That's right. Nothing's confirmed." He fidgeted. "But there's another problem. Purser Mueller just finished inventory. We weren't able to restock in Cuba. We only have food and water for twelve days."

"That's not enough to get us back to Europe, is it?" David said, "We'll have to land somewhere."

"We could make it if we rationed. But if we do have to turn back across the Atlantic, we can't wait long. Don't say anything. The captain's afraid passengers will mutiny. There's already been talk."

"Turn back?" I said, fear clutching my throat.

"Mutiny?" David said.

"We can't turn back!" I exchanged a worried look with David. "Not to Germany. How long do we have?"

The Double Crossing

"I don't know. If you disembark in the next few days, there won't be a problem. Captain Schroeder is determined to find a place for you."

"Why would anyone mutiny?" asked David. "What good would it do? We still wouldn't have a place to land."

"Exactly," Leo said. "Nothing would be accomplished. But some of the passengers are becoming desperate."

• • •

The passenger committee posted a notice about the telegram from HAPAG. People debated the advantages of the Dominican Republic and Cuba, which was still a possibility. The pendulum swung again. Hope returned.

The ship had circled so far north we could see the coast of Florida in the distance. David took turns with me looking through the binoculars.

• • •

At dinner, David's father said, "I heard the passenger committee sent a couple of telegrams to the U.S., to President Roosevelt, asking for his help."

"Roosevelt will surely let us land. We're so close," Frau Jantzen said.

Everyone smiled. I felt a weight lift.

30

MS *St. Louis*, Caribbean
Sunday, June 4 – Monday, June 5

HANNAH

From the deck on Sunday morning, I could see the buildings of Miami, even without binoculars. David stood beside me, our arms brushing at times. Fishing boats came close enough that we saw people on some of them taking pictures of the *St. Louis*.

David waved at men in a passing boat and they waved back. Then a larger boat approached. He peered at it through his binoculars.

"It's the U.S. Coast Guard."

"Do you think they've come to welcome us? Or to keep us from landing?"

"I hope it's to guide us in," David said.

I noticed Otto Schiendick at the rail nearby. "Schiendick doesn't seem happy to see them."

The Nazi steward was staring intently, tapping his fingers on the railing, eyes fixed on the approaching boat. Suddenly he darted away, climbed to the bridge deck, and pushed his way into the radio room.

The Double Crossing

"He must think he can just barge in there, since he's the head Nazi," I said.

"Maybe he's afraid the Americans are after him," David said. "Those documents are supposed to contain information about the U.S. military."

"Oh, I hope so! If they come on board, we'll tell them exactly where to find the papers."

I kept an eye on the door of the radio room and saw First Officer Ostermeyer go inside. A moment later Schiendick came out, red in the face.

"Ostermeyer must have kicked him out," I said.

Schiendick vaulted down the ladder and rushed to the rail again. He ripped off his hat and rubbed his scalp, staring at the cutter, now a lot closer to the *St. Louis*. He started toward the stairway to the lower decks, turned around and came back to look again. Another steward joined him and appeared to ask him something. I recognized Heinrich, Schiendick's cabin-mate.

The Coast Guard boat began to circle the *St. Louis*. Officers on her deck watched us through binoculars. Schiendick and the other steward were having a hushed but animated conversation. I caught the words, "get the box?"

"Maybe he'll throw it overboard," I said. "But I hope they catch him with it and arrest him."

Schiendick gripped the rail, looking from the boat to the stairs and back, seeming undecided. Then the Coast Guard cutter veered away from the *St. Louis*. One of the officers waved and smiled. The watching passengers began waving back. As the boat withdrew, even Schiendick and his friend raised their hands.

"Oh, too bad," I said. "I guess they weren't after the papers."

"Or coming to guide us in," said David. "They're probably staying close to make sure we don't try to land."

My brief moment of hope vanished.

• • •

David took my hand. "Let's go somewhere more private."

Arriving at our lifeboat, David scuffed the toe of his shoe on the deck and fidgeted.

"What did you want to talk about?" I finally asked.

"Um, okay. You know I really like you. And … um … I've never liked a girl before. Not this way." He cleared his throat. "After this thing with Schiendick is over, even if we can't stop him … we'll still be friends, right?"

I relaxed. Poor David. He seemed so miserable. I took his hand. "Of course. I really like you too. Whatever happens, it won't change how I feel about you."

I looked up into his face. He bent toward me and surprised me with a quick kiss. When he pulled back his face was bright red.

"I'm sorry. I didn't ask first. Was that okay?"

"I liked it."

He reached out and lightly twirled one of my curls around his fingers, a silly smile on his face.

For that moment, I forgot the rumbling of the engines taking us farther from Cuba. My first kiss.

• • •

Through Sunday and again on Monday, the *St. Louis* circled near the Florida coast, sometimes close enough to see the buildings of Miami, or the city lights at night. Close enough to shore that gulls followed the ship. Much of the time, U.S. Coast Guard boats also followed the ship.

I couldn't help feeling angry and hurt. It looked like the United States didn't want us either.

David distracted us both by watching gulls through his binoculars and pointing out different species. "I wish we could use Captain Schroeder's books. Some of these gulls are new to me," he said.

"We'd better not bother him," I said. "He has enough to deal with."

The Double Crossing

Small planes often flew over us. Rumor had it they were reporters from U.S. newspapers. Apparently, there was still a lot in the papers about the *St. Louis* and her passengers.

As the hours went on with no definite news, the tension on the ship rose. Everyone was anxious for word from Cuba or from the U.S. government.

The passenger committee kept posting news and rumors, copies of telegrams they'd sent, and some received by the captain. Nothing seemed certain. I checked the boards frequently. One telegram from a rich New York philanthropist read:

```
URGE YOU SAIL INTO INTERNATIONAL ZONE NEAR BEDLOES
ISLAND IN NEW YORK HARBOR AND STAY THERE WHILE I AND
GROUP OF OTHER AMERICAN BUSINESSMEN MEET ALL YOUR
COSTS WHILE AT THE SAME TIME MAKING APPEAL TO
CONGRESS FOR ASYLUM ALL YOUR PASSENGERS
```

At least there were some people in the world who would welcome us.

A note below it said the captain had cabled back and asked the group to make arrangements with HAPAG in New York.

People standing by the message board began talking excitedly. Someone said, "Don't get your hopes up. It's not official."

• • •

Late Monday afternoon, Ruth and I were lying in deck chairs when I felt the ship change course. The engines grew louder. The ship picked up speed and seemed to forge ahead with a purpose.

We jumped up and rushed to the rail.

"We're moving away from the Florida coast," said Ruth.

"South? Back to Cuba?"

Before long a crowd at the bulletin board drew us over. A member of the passenger committee was posting a new notice. Cuba had offered to allow us to land on the Isle of Pines, Cuba's second largest island. We were heading there with all speed.

The crowd cheered. I hugged Ruth.

A couple of Ruth's friends pulled at her sleeve. "C'mon Ruth. Everyone's going to the aft deck to celebrate."

Ruth dragged me along. Young men and women and some children were dancing and roughhousing. There wasn't a band, but the dancers didn't seem to notice.

I stood a little way back and watched. Ruth was swept up in the dancing. She and her friends held hands and reeled around, skirts flying. Ruth's dark hair came loose and blew behind her.

Catching sight of David, I waved. He pushed over to me and swung me around a couple of times.

"Isn't it wonderful? I heard we'll be there by nine tomorrow morning. Mama cried when she heard."

I was a little breathless. "Yes. It's wonderful. And the passengers with families in Cuba will be able to join them."

Dinner was a celebration. I went to bed feeling more light-hearted than I had in days, Until I remembered Schiendick and his box.

I made a decision, shivering under the covers at the idea. But it would be simpler, and I could do it. When everyone was at breakfast, I'd steal the box. I didn't need to tell David. We'd be off the ship before Schiendick noticed it was missing. He wouldn't be able to do anything to me.

31

MS *ST. LOUIS*, CARIBBEAN
TUESDAY, JUNE 6, 1939

DAVID

REBEKAH AND I had repacked our bags for the 9:00 a.m. arrival to the Isle of Pines. When I went on the deck the sun was just over the Eastern horizon and the water shimmered with colors. The ship was moving slowly, and there was no land in sight.

I saw Leo taking the stairs down from the bridge deck and rushed to catch him.

"Why have we slowed down?"

"The captain's meeting with the passenger committee now. He got a telegram from the Cuban office about an hour ago. The Isle of Pines is not confirmed."

"What does that mean?" His words made no sense. I couldn't think clearly.

"It means we don't know. We're waiting again."

This was crazy!

"I've got to go. Sorry. Hopefully it will be cleared up soon." He hurried across the deck.

The Double Crossing

Would Hannah have noticed the ship had slowed down? I hesitated, hating to give her the bad news, but headed downstairs for her cabin. Before I reached it, her door opened and she stepped out. Her hair looked wilder than usual. She glanced nervously up the corridor away from me, then back in my direction. When she caught sight of me, she seemed startled.

"Oh, David! It's you." She fidgeted with a bag she carried.

"Where are you going?"

She flushed, looking embarrassed.

"Umm ... nowhere," she said, not looking at me.

"Come on, Hannah. What's up?"

"I ... I'm going to get the box." She glanced around again. "I'm going to get it and throw it overboard before we land." Now she gave me a defiant look that seemed to say, Don't try to stop me.

"Now? But ... why didn't you tell me? We're supposed to be in this together."

"I thought it would be easier to just do it. I know you aren't keen on the idea." She looked everywhere but at me.

"Well, you should've told me. If you get caught, Schiendick and his goons could throw you overboard and no one would even know." I kept looking at her until she met my eyes again.

"Don't try to talk me out of it! I just want to get it over with. I have to stop him! You can help if you want." She gave me another stubborn look.

"Okay. I do understand. But we can't do it now! We might be on the ship for a long time. We might not be going to the Isle of Pines." I told her what Leo said.

"Oh, not again! Why? Why does this keep happening?" She sat down right there in the corridor, her back against the wall, and started to cry.

I eased myself down beside her. I was hurt, even mad at her, but, seeing her tears, I forgot all that. I put an arm around her.

"I was so ... scared," she stammered, her face streaked with tears. "But I was ready. And now ... another delay?"

After a few minutes she stood up, wiping her eyes. "Maybe we can't do it now, but I'm still going to. Before we land."

"At least tell me first. Let me help."

She didn't answer. The determined look on her face worried me.

• • •

Late in the afternoon, I was perched on the edge of a deck chair, too worried to settle. I wasn't even pretending to watch for birds. All I could think of was whether Hannah was going to get herself in trouble, and about what was going to happen to us all. The ship was circling again. Even though there had been no announcements, everyone realized there was another problem. People were restless and jumpy.

That's where Aaron Pozner found me. His hair had grown during the weeks on the ship. He ran a hand through it, making it stick up in short spikes.

"David, I was looking for you. How are you holding up?"

"I'm okay." It felt like I had a nest of wasps buzzing inside my head.

Pozner slumped into the chair beside mine.

"Listen, I've been talking with some of the other men. About a dozen of us have decided to take action if we have to." Eyes blazing behind his glasses, he leaned toward me. "We're not going to let them take us back to Germany. If the *St. Louis* heads back, we'll take over the ship. I hope you'll be with us."

I was too surprised to answer. He must have thought I was older than almost fourteen, probably because I'm tall.

"I … I couldn't. I mean … it's brave of you and … but, I've talked to Captain Schroeder. I'm friends with Leo, his steward. The captain will do everything to land us somewhere. He's not going to take us back to Germany."

Pozner shook his head. "I hope you're right. I like Leo. He's a good guy. But I don't trust the captain. He never talks to us. I mean, he's treated us well. But he's a German officer. I know what they're capable of."

"If you take over the ship, what good will it do? If no country lets us land?"

"It will show the world how desperate we are. Maybe then someone will take us in. Think about it, David. But keep it to yourself."

"I will." I wouldn't tell, but I wasn't going to join a mutiny against the captain.

Pozner stood. As he walked away, he seemed more like the schoolteacher he'd been than the leader of a mutiny. Suddenly, I had an idea. We could tell Pozner about Schiendick and Operation Sunshine! He was the kind of person we needed on our side. He was a grown-up and if he was willing to lead a mutiny, he wouldn't be afraid of Schiendick and his men. I almost ran after him, but I needed to check with Hannah first.

• • •

No one made announcements the rest of the day. People paced the decks, sweating and fanning themselves, grumbling and asking why we weren't landing on the Isle of Pines. Some passengers huddled in deck chairs, stunned or crying. Fear was contagious. It was impossible to settle down. I walked the ship, unable to concentrate.

32

MS *St. Louis*, Caribbean
Wednesday, June 7 – Thursday, June 8

DAVID

THE SHIP PICKED UP SPEED and turned north again. The captain still hadn't made an announcement. Neither had the passenger committee. Where were we going? Some people said we were headed to New York, to accept the offer from the Jewish philanthropist. Some believed we were going back to Havana, or another Central American port. I even heard whispers that we were being taken back to Germany.

Across the dining saloon at breakfast, a couple raised their voices, arguing so loud everyone could hear. The man stood up, scraping his chair legs across the floor, shouting, "Stop worrying about your mother! We'll let her know as soon as we can!"

His wife jumped up so suddenly that her chair fell back with a crash like a gunshot. She ran from the dining saloon, sobbing. He followed, calling, "Wait. I'm sorry."

After a stunned silence, passengers' voices filled the saloon.

"What's wrong? Why are they so mad?" Rebekah had tears in her eyes.

"Don't worry, *Liebling*," Mama said. "People are just upset and nervous."

• • •

Hannah followed me out of the dining saloon. "I can't stand this. I'm going to spend the day in my room with a book."

"I'm too fidgety to stay inside," I said. "I'll try to find out what's going on."

"Come and tell me if you do. I'll talk to you later." She turned and headed toward the stairs.

I spent most of the day pacing the decks but didn't learn anything until Leo came down from the bridge deck and joined me at the rail.

"I've been hoping to see you," I said. "What's happening? No one knows where we're headed."

"It's not good." Leo looked like he'd swallowed something bitter. "Late last night Captain Schroeder got a message. Negotiations with Cuba are off. Then he got a cable from HAPAG. They're ordering us back to Germany."

I could hardly breathe. "But, you said ... The captain said he'd find us a place to land!"

"He was hoping something else would work out. That's why he waited to tell the passenger committee."

"But ... what about the rich man in New York? Or that other island? There must be something else we can do."

Was this the end for us? Would we go to a concentration camp, like Pozner? My breath felt stuck in my throat.

"The New York offer wasn't confirmed. Neither were any of the others. We can't keep circling. We'll run out of food and fuel. This afternoon, the captain told the committee that we're headed back."

Leo looked at me and put a hand on my arm. "It isn't over. Negotiations are going on in Europe. We're hoping to land in England."

"The passenger committee hasn't posted anything. Why haven't they told us?"

"Perhaps they were too discouraged to face the passengers right away. The Propaganda Ministry in Germany is using this to justify the Nazi's treatment of Jews."

He handed me a piece of paper. "This came over the wireless, from an article in the German press about the *St. Louis*. Look at this paragraph." He pointed halfway down the page.

> Was it we who sent them off to Cuba? Was it we who denied them the right to work in France? Is it our fault that Australia, Canada, the U.S.A., Sumatra, and God knows who else refuse to let the Panic Party land? No, it was the democratic nations who are using the Jews in a game of political chess against the Reich.

Leo pointed farther down the page:

> Jews are our misfortune ... we have to house them because no one else will have them.

"Did they stage the whole thing for propaganda? I mean, this whole voyage?" I was sick to my stomach.

"I don't know, but either way, they've taken advantage of it. Captain Schroeder is furious. The party used him."

"And all of us." I couldn't look at Leo, afraid of bursting into tears. "Well ... good night. Thanks." I choked out the words and went straight to my cabin. I couldn't face telling my family, or Hannah. They'd all know soon.

• • •

The next morning, an announcement over the loudspeakers asked all passengers to assemble in the social hall for an important meeting. I sat with my family, Hannah and Ruth. A rumble of conversation filled the hall as passengers waited for everyone to arrive. Knowing what was coming, I reached for Hannah's hand.

The Double Crossing

Josef Joseph stood on the platform, looking old. The hall got quiet. He made the announcement: "Friends and fellow passengers. I must inform you that the *St. Louis* is heading back to Europe."

Gasps from the audience. Someone shouted, "To Germany?"

The hall filled with moans and cries.

"Please. No!"

"This can't happen!"

Hannah went rigid. Her hand squeezed mine so hard it hurt.

"Quiet please, everyone!" Herr Joseph shouted, "It doesn't necessarily mean returning to Germany. Let's stay calm. Negotiations are underway."

His words were almost lost in the uproar. A noisy group of young men pushed one man forward. It was Aaron Pozner.

Pozner joined Joseph at the front of the social hall. His voice rang out strong. His words got everyone's attention.

"We cannot go back to Germany! Some of us were let out of concentration camps with the warning that we had to leave the country forever. To return means one thing—being sent back to those camps! That could also be the future of every man, woman, and child on this ship!"

Pandemonium broke out. Everyone talked at once. Hannah leaned into me, crying. Ruth, on the other side, put an arm around her. Mama held Rebekah, who was crying too.

Someone began to chant and soon everyone joined in. "*Wir dürfen nicht sterben ... Wir kommen nicht wieder ... Wir dürfen nicht sterben!*" We must not die ... we will not return ... we must not die!

Another man from the passenger committee came forward. His booming voice silenced the crowd.

"Ladies and gentlemen, the news is bad. But Europe is still many days away. That gives the Joint, and all our friends, time to help us. This rash behavior will accomplish nothing. The committee welcomes any practical suggestions."

A man jumped to his feet. "People could take turns throwing themselves overboard. The ship would have to stop to rescue them. It would slow us down."

"Good idea! We'll choose the best swimmers," said another man.

The man on the platform said, "That's as foolhardy a suggestion as I've heard. It would accomplish nothing."

I thought so too, but he had asked for suggestions.

The two men who'd spoken up stormed angrily out of the social hall, followed by Pozner and his group.

No other suggestions were made. The rest of the passengers left in small groups, grumbling and agonizing among themselves.

"Will we have to go to a concentration camp like he said? What will they do to us?" Rebekah whimpered.

Mama tried to reassure her. "Don't worry. They'll find another country for us."

"They keep talking about negotiations," Hannah said, sounding almost as scared as Rebekah. "Are they just trying to shut us up?"

When we were on the deck by ourselves, I told Hannah about the news article Leo showed me. "He and the captain think the Nazis have used this whole voyage for propaganda. But I don't believe the captain will take us back to Germany."

Hannah crossed her arms, her face flushed. "Well, at least there's one thing I can do to fight back!" She said goodbye, turned, and hurried away.

I wanted to follow her, to remind her not to try to get the documents from Schiendick without telling me, but she rushed off, and Leo caught up to me, pale and scowling.

"How are the passengers taking the news?"

"Everyone's terrified we're going back to Germany."

"The captain won't let that happen. Listen, I have news too. Captain Schroeder received a cable this morning from HAPAG in Hamburg. The police are investigating my 'family background.'

The captain was ordered to clarify my background and radio back immediately."

"Oh, no! Was it Schiendick?"

"Must have been. Captain showed me the cable, and his reply. 'God help us both if they discover the truth,' he said. He'd written, *Fullest questioning reveals steward Jockl loyal to party and country. No evidence of Semitic background.*

"He didn't let me down. He's a good man, David. He won't let his passengers down either."

As we stared at each other, the loudspeaker boomed with another announcement. "By order of the ship's *Nationalsozialisten* Party leader, there is now a ban on any further social interaction between crew members and passengers. Crewmen will associate with passengers only in the performance of their duties."

Leo and I looked at each other in shock.

"Schiendick couldn't have had the captain's authority for that. He must have pulled party rank on Purser Mueller. Well, I'd better get back to the performance of my duties."

"Thanks for all your help, Leo. I guess we won't be able to keep talking like this. I hope the Captain's cable is enough to stop that so-called investigation."

Leo walked away, his shoulders slumped. He didn't look like the same enthusiastic steward who'd befriended us a couple of weeks ago.

Part Four

33

MS *St. Louis*, Atlantic Ocean
Thursday, June 8

HANNAH

I PRETENDED TO BE ASLEEP when Ruth went out. What was the point of going to breakfast? Did the Nazis know all along that we'd be sent back? How treacherous of them to put us through this whole *rigmarole* (an English word). My thoughts whirled like a caged squirrel. I'd been awake most of the night.

Mother must know the *St. Louis* was turned back. People said newspapers all over the world were full of the story. The Nazis used it to prove no one wanted Jews. She must be frantic with worry.

If the *St. Louis* took us back to Hamburg, the Gestapo, or the *Schutzstaffel* (SS) in their black uniforms, might be waiting at the dock to send us all to concentration camps. My mind went to the last time I saw my father, his face bruised, and coat torn, paraded out of Oldenburg with the rest of the town's Jewish men. The more I heard about those camps, the more I was afraid for Father. If he was still alive, why hadn't he come back with the others?

The Double Crossing

I promised myself I'd stop Schiendick, before they had a chance to send me to a camp, or I'd die trying. It was the only thing I could do to fight the Nazis. For Father, even if he'd never know.

• • •

The tourist class dining saloon was gloomy and quiet at lunch. Ruth and I sat by ourselves. We were early and David's family hadn't arrived yet.

The steward handed each of us a mimeographed sheet of paper.

"What's this?" Ruth asked. "Where's the regular menu?"

Instead of the printed lunch menu, offering several entrees, it was a fixed menu, with no choices.

"I apologize. We're facing a food shortage. We had to leave Havana without restocking."

"What happened to our luxury cruise?" Ruth said after he left. It wasn't like her to be sarcastic.

I wasn't in the mood for breakfast anymore. "It doesn't matter to me. I'm not hungry."

"Don't be discouraged, Hannah." Ruth put her hand over mine on the table. "They'll find somewhere for us. People are pretty sure England will take us."

"They said President Roosevelt would let us in. But he never even answered the telegrams. It's true what the Nazis are saying. No one wants us."

I threw down my napkin, pushed back my chair, and stood up.

"I'm sorry. I don't want to start crying in front of everyone. I can't eat anyway."

Why had I allowed myself to be happy on the *St. Louis*? How could I have believed this Nazi ship would take us to freedom?

• • •

The air was fresh and cooler on the deck now that we were in the Atlantic again. I leaned on the rail, took some deep breaths, and gazed at the open sea. Only a few high white clouds skimmed overhead, interrupting the blue.

I thought of home. The beautiful polished oak dining table where we ate our meals and celebrated Passovers. Mother had had to sell it for almost nothing, along with the rest of our furniture, when we were forced to move. I pictured my cozy upstairs bedroom, the window seat where I sat to read. I'd lived there all my life.

I jumped at the sound of David's voice.

"Are you all right? Sorry. I didn't mean to startle you."

The concern in his eyes brought on my tears.

"I'm afraid. I might never see Mother and Father. I can't face a concentration camp. I won't be able to stand it."

"You won't have to. Captain Schroeder's not going to take us to Germany. I trust him."

I wished I felt as certain.

• • •

At dinner with the Jantzens, David's father was optimistic. "Herr Joseph, from the passenger committee, said that many passengers have pooled the last of their money, even sold valuables to crew members, to pay for one more round of telegrams. I gave him the little money I had left." He looked at Frau Jantzen.

"I'm glad you did."

He smiled at her. "Tomorrow the committee is going to sit in the radio room and cable all the important heads of government in England, France, Belgium, and Holland, and religious and civic leaders throughout Europe. Herr Joseph is convinced they'll listen to our pleas and take us in."

I said a prayer in my mind that he was right.

• • •

That evening, as darkness fell, I walked around the ship with David. An orchestra played in the social hall and a movie was being shown in the cinema, but both places were practically deserted. Few people were even on the deck.

"It's a sad ship now. Not like when we were on our way to Cuba," David said.

We walked along in silence for a while. "There's something I've been wanting to tell you," David said. "You know Aaron Pozner, who spoke in front of the meeting?"

"I know who he is. You said he'd been in a concentration camp." I remembered how angry he'd been at the meeting. "He was the one who said we'll all end up in the camps if we go back to Germany."

"Right. He has a group of about a dozen guys." He stopped walking. We were near our lifeboat. He pulled me over beside it. "Don't tell anyone else, okay?"

"Sure. Tell what?"

"Pozner and the others are planning to take over the ship, to stop them from taking us back to Germany."

"You mean mutiny? Why? How would that get us anywhere?"

"I told him it wouldn't help. And I'm sure the captain isn't going to take us to Germany. But … if these guys aren't afraid to try something like that, I bet they wouldn't be afraid of Schiendick and his firemen."

His eyes shone with excitement. "Here's my idea. We should get Pozner's help! Especially now that we can't ask Leo."

I tensed. "Wait. What are you saying?"

"Pozner and his men could help us stop Shiendick!"

"What do you think they could do?" I said.

"Well, I'm not sure, but …"

Pozner had been in a camp like Father. He was already taking a big risk with this mutiny idea. He should stay away from Schiendick.

"I don't know, David."

Stopping Schiendick was my fight against the Nazis. I still had the key to Schiendick's cabin. I had a plan. I didn't need anyone else besides David involved. Maybe not even him.

I shook my head. "Don't tell Pozner yet."

34

MS *St. Louis*, Atlantic Ocean
Friday, June 9

DAVID

Papa and I were on deck together, each of us holding our binoculars. We hadn't caught sight of any birds, not even a little storm petrel. When I heard loud voices nearby, I looked over to see a couple of crewmen speaking to a group of passengers. They were some of Schiendick's Gestapo agents. When they walked away, the passengers had shocked looks on their faces. The crewmen came swaggering toward us. I tensed, remembering what they did to Pozner.

Standing threateningly close to Papa, one of them said, "By order of our *Ortsgruppenleiter*, we've come to inform you that these are your last free days. Enjoy them. After we return to Hamburg, none of you will be heard of again."

I clenched my fists, wanting to hit the guy for talking to Papa like that.

"We shall see," Papa said, resting a steadying hand on my arm.

The Double Crossing

"You'll see what it's like to have your head shaved in *Dachau!*" The crewmen laughed. They turned and walked toward another group of passengers.

"Those are Otto Schiendick's men." I was boiling inside. "Now that he thinks we're going back to Germany, that gestapo thug is going behind Captain Schroeder's back."

"It's all right son. It's empty talk. Still, I'm going to check on Rebekah and your mother. I don't want them frightened."

I worried Schiendick's goons would try to rough up Pozner again. Then I caught sight of Pozner himself, heading up the stairs to the bridge deck with a group of young men.

I watched them push through the door onto the bridge. They must be making their move! Would there be gunshots? I waited, and waited, barely breathing, my eyes on that door, expecting shouts, or crewmen to come running.

Then Captain Schroeder came marching along the upper deck, looking like an angry rooster. He flung open the door and disappeared into the bridge. Now the fireworks would start!

I paced and fidgeted, watching the bridge door until it opened again. Pozner and the other men filed out quietly. They came down the stairs, spoke briefly to one another, and went off in different directions. There had been no alarms. No shots fired.

I hurried to catch up with Pozner just as he reached the stairs to the lower decks.

"I saw you go onto the bridge. What happened?"

"Come with me to my cabin." He seemed jumpy, glancing around as we descended each level.

"Sit down, David." He pointed to the only chair in the cabin and sat heavily onto his bunk with a sigh.

"We took over the bridge with no problems. There were only three officers, and we overpowered them. We made them send for Captain Schroeder." He stared at his hands, which gripped each other in his lap.

"What did the captain do?"

"He asked us what we hoped to achieve. I told him we wanted to save our lives. We were taking over the ship to sail it to any country other than Germany.

"He said, 'I'm sure the other passengers won't support you. You don't control the engine room. My crew will overpower you.'

"I guess we didn't think it through very well. One of my men threatened that we'd use the captain as a hostage. But Schroeder just said, 'I will give no order, no matter what you do, that will take my ship off course. Without that, you can do nothing.'"

"Captain Schroeder isn't someone to be bullied," I said.

"He told us we could be charged with piracy, and if that happened, we'd be taken back to Germany to stand trial. He said he sympathized with us. He gave us one minute to leave the bridge with a promise not to try to take over the ship again, and he wouldn't press charges."

"So you did?"

"After he promised he'd do everything in his power to land us in England. That seemed the best we could hope for. We gave him our word not to try again, and we left."

Pozner looked straight at me for the first time since beginning his story. "You trust him, right? Do you think he'll do what he said?"

"I'm sure he will. He's an honorable man."

• • •

Later that afternoon I'd just finished telling Hannah about Pozner's attempt to take over the ship when the loudspeaker announced a meeting for all the passengers. The captain would address us for the first time.

"Do you think it's about the mutiny?"

"I don't think so. But it's good he's finally going to talk to everyone himself."

When we got there, the social hall was packed. Captain Schroeder was standing on the platform under the portrait of

Hitler. He spoke in a calm voice, telling everyone that he understood our problem and fears. His speech was short, but he seemed so confident that the tension began to dissolve.

"I assure you, no matter what happens, I will not return you to Germany," he said.

As we were leaving the meeting, Papa and Mama caught up with us. Papa patted me on the back. "I like your friend the captain. I believe he'll do as he says. Hopefully we can join Aunt Retta's family in England soon, and stay there until our number comes up for the United States."

Mama took my hand and smiled with relief.

35

MS *St. Louis*, Atlantic Ocean
Saturday, June 10 – Monday, June 12

DAVID

I STILL SPENT most of my time on deck. It was better than being cooped up in the cramped cabin. And there was always a chance I might spot another huge flock of birds. I often caught sight of fulmars, petrels, or shearwaters, and never tired of watching them fly and feed, but only one or two birds at a time, not a big flock like before.

The fresh sea breeze was a welcome break from smells of the hundreds of unwashed people on the ship. There wasn't enough water now for laundry. Showers were rationed. To keep from running out of food and water, everything was limited. Meals were skimpy and boring. No fresh eggs or fruit, few vegetables, and no choices.

Like the birds flying over the ocean, rumors flew on board. Papa had heard that a man named Morris Troper, who represented the American Joint Distribution Committee in Europe, was negotiating with several countries to divide up the passengers. I didn't care which country we went to, as long as Hannah went there too.

The Double Crossing

But Hannah was avoiding me. Even when we were together, she was quiet, not her usual talkative self. I didn't know if she was angry, or what. It felt like she'd closed herself off from me, and it hurt.

On Monday morning, I'd finally caught up to her and we'd walked to our spot by the lifeboat. The sea was calm and the ship seemed to be making good time. A briny-smelling breeze ruffled our hair.

"So, um, can we talk?" I said, my skimpy breakfast suddenly a lump in my stomach.

"What about?"

"You know ... Pozner and—"

"I don't want him to take over!" The tension between us broke like a thunderstorm. "Besides, it would be more dangerous for him, with his mutiny and all. I just want to wait until we're closer, so we can be off the ship before Schiendick misses the box." Her mouth was set in a stubborn line and her eyes shone like green fire.

"Please, Hannah, I think we need help."

"No! We can do this. You can't look at the world through binoculars, like you're watching from far away. This is our real life. This affects us. You haven't had your family taken away. Hitler has to be stopped!"

Why was she attacking me? My throat tightened, like in the school office in Hamburg, staring at the Nazi swastika badge on the Director's lapel when he kicked me out of school. The name he called me rang in my head: Abomination! Abomination!

"David, are you all right? That was harsh. I'm sorry."

I shook my head to clear the memory. "I do see what's going on. We're in this together. We're friends, right? You can count on me."

"It's just ..." Hannah swallowed. Her eyes shone with tears. "They've taken everything from me. I hate the Nazis! Schiendick is a bully, like the ones who destroyed Father's store and took him away. This is my chance to do something."

"I know." I patted her shoulder, feeling awkward. Her back tensed, then relaxed.

"I understand how you feel. But, in case we need help, is it okay if I tell Pozner?"

She stepped back. "If you do, tell him not to interfere. Tell him we'll handle it."

"Yeah. Okay. But, like you say, we will handle it. Both of us." I was afraid of what Schiendick might do if he caught her breaking into his cabin alone, but bit back the words. She was upset enough already.

• • •

That afternoon I was on A deck when I saw Leo coming toward me. We hadn't spoken since Schiendick's order banning "social interaction" between passengers and crew.

"I'm glad I found you alone. Come over here." He pulled me to a deserted spot near the stern. "I don't want any of Schiendick's guys to see me with you."

"What is it?"

"Captain Schroeder is relieved. Things look promising for you all to be taken in by friendly countries."

I felt my shoulders relax. I didn't realize how tense I'd been.

"But there's something I want to tell you," Leo went on in a whisper. "No one else can know. Not until the Nazis are out of power. But someday, everyone should know. He has a plan. In case we're ordered back to Germany. He probably won't have to carry it out."

He leaned close and spoke into my ear. "Last night, after the passenger meeting, the captain called in the purser and chief engineer. I heard him tell them that if all else fails, he plans to run the *St. Louis* aground close to the southern coast of England, set her on fire, and evacuate everyone ashore. It has to be kept secret from everyone else. To make it seem an accident."

"Honestly? He would do that for us?"

"Yes, but he probably won't have to. When all this is over, and it won't put him in danger, I hope you'll tell people what a good

The Double Crossing

man he is. He knows how desperate things are for the Jews and detests what the Nazis are doing. He'll keep his promise not to take you back to Germany."

• • •

Monday night, Purser Mueller managed to come up with a film we hadn't seen yet, a comedy. My family joined the stream of people filing into the cinema. I felt more relaxed with Hannah since our talk. She sat with us. When one of the characters said, "Traveling by sea makes one nervous," the room exploded in laughter.

36

MS *St. Louis*, Atlantic Ocean
Tuesday, June 13 – Thursday, June 15

HANNAH

IT WAS GOOD David and I had talked. I felt close to him again. He understood and would back me up with Schiendick. But as I looked in the tiny bathroom mirror, trying to brush tangles out of my hair, I realized that I hadn't been totally honest about my feelings.

It wasn't right to drag David into something dangerous when he was probably only doing it as my friend. If only I hadn't agreed to let him tell Pozner. That man might do something crazy, like when he tried to lead a mutiny. If Schiendick got suspicious, he might hide the documents somewhere else.

It was a terrifying thought, but it would be best for me to sneak in and take the box by myself. It might be easier for one person alone. And if I got caught, I'd be the only one hurt. I should act before Pozner could meddle.

• • •

Wednesday at breakfast they announced another meeting of all the passengers. Captain Schroeder would be there.

"This must be it," Herr Jantzen said. "Now we'll find out where we're going."

Everyone seemed on edge, expecting to hear the decisions that would determine our future lives.

At ten a.m., we all waited eagerly in the crowded hall. Joseph Josef stepped onto the platform and announced that the passenger committee had received a telegram from Morris Troper the evening before. He read it aloud:

```
FINAL ARRANGEMENT FOR DISEMBARKATION ALL PASSENGERS
COMPLETE. GOVERNMENTS OF BELGIUM, HOLLAND, FRANCE,
AND ENGLAND COOPERATED MAGNIFICENTLY WITH AMERICAN
JOINT DISTRIBUTION COMMITTEE TO EFFECT THIS
POSSIBILITY.
```

The hall erupted with cheers. People cried and hugged each other. After a moment, Herr Josef asked for silence. He thanked Captain Schroeder and his crew for helping make possible our delivery to safety. The captain, looking pleased and relieved, was on the platform with Herr Josef. He smiled and nodded but didn't speak.

I clapped my hands with everyone else, cheered, and hugged Ruth.

After we filed out of the social hall, Ruth dashed off to find her friends. I went to our cabin alone. I paced up and down the tiny room, twisting and untwisting a lock of hair.

It was time to act. Was I brave enough to do it alone? It was just as dangerous with both of us, so why involve David? And I didn't want to wait until he dragged Pozner into it.

Tomorrow morning. I'd sneak into Schiendick's room, steal the metal box, and throw it overboard. With luck, it would all be over in a few minutes and no one would know.

That evening a celebration party was held. Singers, magicians, a classical pianist, and comedians performed. Everyone laughed a lot. But what got the most laughs was when one of the comedians read from the HAPAG brochure, *On the* St. Louis, *one travels securely, and lives in comfort with everything one can wish for to make life on board a pleasure.* You had to either laugh or cry at the contrast, after crossing most of the Atlantic on meager rations, with no clean clothes, and few baths.

I joined in the laughter, almost doubling over. It was something that would only be funny to this group of people. That thought made me laugh even more, until I was almost hysterical, tears in my eyes. Weeks of tension seemed to drain from the room.

But when everyone quieted down, wiping our eyes and still smiling, I thought about tomorrow. The *kopfkino*, movie in my head, began playing. Vivid scenes played as I pictured all the things that might go wrong.

• • •

In the morning I went to breakfast early and finished quickly. I caught a glimpse of David as I was leaving but avoided running into him. He might guess my plan if he saw my face. This was my mission against the Nazis.

I left my cabin with the empty bag over my shoulder, fingering the key in my pocket with hands that shook. The key Leo had stolen for us, that I'd never given back. Since I didn't know Schiendick's schedule, I hung around the tourist class passageway watching for him, trying not to look nervous. Before long, a man in a white steward's jacket came out of a nearby cabin, carrying a bucket of cleaning supplies. It was him. He disappeared into another cabin.

On legs that felt like jelly, I hurried aft toward the crew quarters. The rumble of the ship's engines echoed the drumming in my chest and reminded me that every moment brought us closer to Europe.

When I reached the door marked NO PASSENGERS BEYOND THIS POINT, I paused. There could be no excuse like being lost this time if I got caught.

The Double Crossing

Seeing no one, I turned the handle and pushed the door open. I could hardly believe my luck. The corridor was empty on that side too! I took a breath and my hand closed again on the room key in my pocket. I rushed to the third door and inserted it into the lock. If Schiendick's roommate was inside, my luck would be over.

I inched open the door and peeked in cautiously. The smell of cigarettes and men's bodies made me wrinkle my nose. The room was empty! The beds were made. The bathroom door, just beyond the bunks that nearly filled the drab room, was closed. It would only take a minute to grab the box and get out.

Then I heard water running in the bathroom! I froze. The roommate! I could still close the door and tiptoe out without being seen. But the box was steps away. Under the bed. I might not get another chance.

I took a shallow breath and crept across the couple of paces to Schiendick's bed. On hands and knees, I thrust my arm underneath and felt along the floor for the box. The water was still running. There it was! A cold metal rectangle pushed up against the back wall. Grabbing it in both hands, I slid it out. I had it!

The cabin was suddenly quiet. I felt the hairs lift on the back of my neck. The water had been turned off. I couldn't breathe. My hands were slippery with sweat. I mustn't drop the box. Pushing myself to my feet, I reached the door in two long steps, slipping the box into my shoulder bag as I went.

"Hey!" came a yell behind me. "Halt! Drop that!"

Without turning to look, I ran out of the cabin and toward the door at the end of the corridor.

Schiendick's roommate yelled after me. Out of the corner of my eye, I saw him in the door of the room, wearing only a towel around his waist. His face burned with anger.

"Halt!" he yelled again.

His bare feet slapped the floor behind me. I pulled open the door to the passenger area, tore through it and down the corridor. The man kept yelling. "Halt! Halt! Thief!" A few curious passengers stuck their heads out of cabins. I dashed for the stairs. All I had to do was get on the deck and toss the box over. I wouldn't think about what might happen after that.

The footsteps behind stopped. I glanced over my shoulder. The man stood in the open door to the crew area, dripping, wearing only the towel. He began shouting, "Schiendick! Hey Otto!"

As I reached the stairs to the next level, I turned and saw Schiendick hurry around a corner into the passageway. His roommate called, "Look! That Jew-girl. She took the box from under your bed!"

"Halt! *Komm zurück!* Bring that back!" Schiendick yelled. "Thief! Halt!" He pounded after me. I raced up the stairs. He was a grown man, but I was fast and he was overweight. Still, by the time I'd run up two flights of stairs to the B deck, he was close behind, both of us gasping for air.

37

MS *St. Louis*, Atlantic Ocean
Thursday, June 15, 1939

DAVID

AARON POZNER AND I rounded a turn in the corridor, on the way to Hannah's cabin. I'd just told Pozner about Schiendick's spy operation and we needed to make a plan with Hannah. If only she didn't get mad again.

Angry voices and running footsteps sounded down the hall. I saw Schiendick hurl himself up the stairs shouting, "Stop! Thief! Come back *Jüdische Diebin!*"

I stopped so suddenly that Pozner bumped into me.

"He's after Hannah!" I shouted, starting to run. "She must have taken the box!"

I sprinted toward the stairs, Pozner on my heels. Schiendick had already reached the next level. I shot up the stairs as fast as I could, heart racing. I was gaining!

When I came out of the stairwell onto the B deck, Hannah was already at the rail. Schiendick was halfway across the deck,

The Double Crossing

racing toward her. Sure enough, she held the metal box in one hand, lifting it over the rail.

"No! Stop!" Schiendick threw himself toward Hannah, shrieking and reaching for the box. She flung it far out, away from the ship and into the ocean.

"No!" Schiendick reached the rail a split second too late. He leaned out to watch the box fall, his face contorted with fury. He looked like a madman.

He turned on Hannah, growling like a dog about to attack, his face the red of the Nazi flag. "I'm going after it! And you're going over with me!" Grabbing Hannah's arm, he wrenched her against him and leaned farther out.

"Let go of me!" Hannah struggled against his grip, her red hair a wild blur around her.

Everything seemed to happen in slow motion. I pumped my legs faster, gulping for air.

"Stop the ship!" Schiendick shouted, clenching Hannah to him.

Hannah gripped the rail with her free hand, grunting and trying to pull away from the infuriated Nazi.

Schiendick hoisted one leg over the side.

Hannah couldn't hold on! I flung myself across the last meter separating us, threw my arms around her waist and pulled.

Pozner reached my side, caught Schiendick's arm, and pried loose his grip on Hannah.

Hannah and I tottered, suddenly released. We fell back, crashing onto the deck. She landed on top of me. We scrambled to help each other up.

Pozner held on while the heavier Schiendick kicked and twisted.

"Take your filthy Jewish hands off me!" the steward screamed. "Someone stop the ship!"

I tried to get to them, but before I could, Schiendick butted Pozner's face with his head. Pozner lurched back, blood spurting from his nose.

The steward threw himself over the rail, shouting as he fell.

Everything felt unreal. A nightmare. Hannah screamed. We all three looked over the rail in time to see Schiendick hit the water far below, sending up a huge splash before disappearing under the churning swell.

Hannah's face was white. Pozner's nose streamed blood.

Several passengers and crew members were already at the rail, alerted by the commotion. A crewman shouted, "Man overboard! Port side!"

Another said, "That was Schiendick. Has he gone crazy?"

Schiendick's head appeared above the dark surface of the water. He paddled weakly, using only one arm, and was falling behind the ship, fighting the roiling water of the wake. I couldn't see the box anymore.

Cries of "Man overboard, port side!" repeated down the deck. A crewman ran for the bridge. Another rushed to the stern with a life preserver and threw it over the rail. Schiendick struggled, thrashed and flailed, and finally grasped it.

Time slowed down. Only minutes had passed since he went over the rail, but it felt like forever.

Someone handed Pozner a handkerchief, which he pressed to his bloody nose.

The water below was almost black and had to be freezing. I gripped Hannah's hand. A horrible vision of Schiendick dragging her down with him, forcing her under the water, replayed in my head.

A single long blast sounded on the ship's horn, the man-overboard signal. A voice over the loudspeaker said, "Man overboard, port side!"

The engine noise changed. The ship began to turn toward the side where we stood. We looked up at the sound of a commotion above on the A deck. Crewmen were lowering a rescue boat.

Passengers and crew leaned over the rail, watching Schiendick, who clung to the life preserver. Voices asked what happened.

The Double Crossing

"Another suicide attempt," said one of the crewmen, shaking his head.

"Hang on, Otto," yelled the sailor who threw the life preserver. "We're coming to get you." I doubted Schiendick could hear him so far below in the water, falling farther behind the ship.

"He almost pulled that girl over the rail with him," said a passenger, holding onto his gray hat and pointing at Hannah. "I saw it."

The rescue boat, smaller than the lifeboats, splashed onto the water with three crewmen aboard. One of the sailors positioned an outboard motor and started it. The boat sped toward Schiendick, well behind the turning ship. When the boat reached him, the other two sailors caught the steward and dragged him aboard. He screamed as they pulled him into the boat.

Schiendick shouted something but I couldn't make out his words.

The crewmen tried to settle him down. The one at the motor started it up again and sped back toward the ship. Schiendick threw himself at him. It looked like he was trying to turn the boat around. He was pulled off, screaming, by another crewman, and collapsed onto a thwart. He yelled and I heard, "... Order! ... *Reich!*"

A crewman sat on either side of him, holding his arms and talking to him, while the boat motored alongside the ship.

Hannah leaned into me, shaking and crying quietly.

"It's going to be all right." I put my arm around her. "They've got him. You did it!" I whispered, "You stopped Operation Sunshine."

She smiled up at me, tears streaming down her face. "I did, didn't I?"

How were we going to keep her safe from Schiendick and his goons for the rest of the trip?

• • •

After the boat was hoisted on board and the rescue completed, the crowd on B deck began to disperse. The engines roared to life and the ship turned back on course. People left in small groups, talking and speculating on why the steward had jumped.

"I'm going to go clean up." Pozner's face and shirt were covered in blood, though the bleeding had stopped.

"Thank you, Aaron. I couldn't have stopped him pulling Hannah over without your help."

Hannah and I were still at the rail. I was shaking and felt her trembling beside me.

"Are you all right, Hannah?" It was Leo, coming across the deck to us. "They're saying he tried to pull you overboard with him."

"I'm fine."

"She's a little shaken up," I said, at the same time.

"Okay. Captain wants to see both of you. He said you have some explaining to do."

"What will he do to us?" I asked.

"I don't know. Dr. Glauner's keeping Schiendick in the infirmary. He's going to be okay. He dislocated his shoulder and had some other injuries. Screamed bloody murder. He told the captain that Hannah stole something valuable, and she had to be taken back to Germany 'to be punished for crimes against the *Reich*.'"

"Oh no! Captain Schroeder won't do that, will he?" I said.

"I knew I was taking a risk." Hannah's voice cracked.

• • •

When we entered his cabin, Captain Schroeder was seated at the desk, looking stern and angry.

Would he have to do what Schiendick demanded? Take her back to Germany to be punished? I couldn't let that happen. My mind whirled. What could I do?

"Explain this to me," the captain said. "I gave you youngsters what I thought was a clear order not to try to interfere with Schiendick's mission. It appears you ignored that order, Hannah. From what I hear, you nearly got yourself and Schiendick killed. What do you have to say?"

The Double Crossing

I rushed to speak first. "Sir. It wasn't just Hannah. I helped. Please don't send her to Germany. She only did what was right."

"Calm down. I'm not sending anyone back to Germany. However, I'm disappointed in the two of you. While I don't doubt you did what you believed was right, you've put me in a difficult position. Hannah, what do you say?"

"I'm sorry about making trouble for you. But I had to do it. No matter what they do to me. And I did it by myself." She gave me a defiant look.

"But—" I began.

Leo interrupted, "I wasn't there, sir. But I helped. I got them a key to Schiendick's room. I also felt it was important—"

"Enough! I'll talk to you later, steward." The captain seemed to deflate. "That man can make a lot of trouble for the two of us, Leo. He's already having you investigated. And he has a long list of complaints against me. Just between us, I'm going to resign after this voyage. I hope that will be enough."

"Sir—" began Leo.

"No, Leo. When I learned from Herr Hoffman that my ship was being used for a spy mission, that decided me. I can't go on representing this government as ship's captain."

I wanted to say something. But what? We hadn't meant to make trouble for Captain Schroeder and Leo.

The captain turned his attention back to us. "I think you two will be safe. Steward Schiendick will remain in the infirmary under watch, 'to prevent another suicide.' And we'll arrive in Antwerp the day after tomorrow. Now tell me, I heard Herr Pozner was involved. What was his role in this venture?"

"I'd only just told him about Operation Sunshine when we saw Schiendick chasing Hannah. Pozner helped me stop him from pulling her overboard. And he got a bloody nose trying to keep Schiendick from jumping."

"I see. Well, I expect to hold you two accountable for your disobedience. I'm not sure how."

"You'll be short a steward," Hannah said. "I could help with cleaning rooms."

"So could I."

Captain Schroeder cleared his throat. He put his hand over his mouth. Hiding a smile? "I appreciate it, but that won't be necessary, or possible. You're both minors, and passengers. I'll speak to your parents, David. Hannah, as yours aren't on board, I'll have a talk with the young woman who's accompanying you. And I'll write a letter for her to give your parents. They'll have to be responsible for discipline."

"Yes, sir," we said, almost in unison.

"Now let me have that key," Captain Schroeder said.

"Sorry, sir." Hannah, her face flushed, reached into her pocket for the key to Schiendick's room and handed it to the captain, with an apologetic look at Leo.

"That will be all," he said. "Leo, I want you to stay."

PART FIVE

38

MS *St. Louis*
Thursday, June 15 – Saturday, June 17

HANNAH

When we left Captain Schroeder, David took my arm and led me toward "our spot."

"What are you thinking, Hannah? How do you feel? Let's go talk."

My mind was racing. So much had happened in the last hour. I was still shaking with fright. I needed to remember I'd stopped Operation Sunshine. That was the most important thing.

I chewed my lip. Would Mother ever see that letter Captain Schroeder was going to write? What would she say? Was she alright? I hoped she'd be proud of me. I'd done something against Hitler. I straightened my back, walking taller.

When we were hidden behind the lifeboat, I said, "You saved my life! If you hadn't been there … I shouldn't have left you out. Thanks for sticking up for me with Captain Schroeder." Just remembering the Nazi leader's hands dragging me up the railing made me start shaking even more.

The Double Crossing

"True, you shouldn't have done it alone. Thank goodness, we got there in time. But ... I have to say ... you were amazing! You did it! You know what's strange? I even felt sorry for Schiendick. He panicked, trying to save that box. I wonder what the Gestapo, or the *Abwehr*, will do to him."

"It's his fault, whatever they do. He's an evil man, working for an evil government. Still, I'm glad I didn't get him killed. Now I'm worried that Leo and Captain Schroeder might be in trouble because of what I did."

"And I'm worried you might not be safe. Even though Schiendick's locked up, word spreads on the ship. We know his roommate saw you. That Gestapo gang will find out what happened and be out for blood. I have an idea though. Pozner and his friends could make sure they don't try anything. I'll ask him."

"But—"

"No buts. We're not taking chances. Just a couple more days until we're out of reach of the Nazis." He put his hands on my shoulders and looked down at me with those intense blue eyes.

"Hannah, I hope we go to the same country. But promise me, if we don't, we'll stay in touch. You'll write to me. We'll see each other again after this is over."

My heart flip-flopped. "Yes. I promise."

David walked with me to my cabin and left me there.

"Remember, don't take any chances," he said. "I'll go talk to Pozner."

Except for meals, I spent the rest of the day in my room. He had me worried.

• • •

The next day before lunch, Ruth burst into our cabin, out of breath.

"Hannah! Guess what! The captain talked to me. He gave me this letter for your parents." She pulled an envelope out of her pocket. It bore the HAPAG insignia. "I can't believe you did that. Tell me how you knew about that Nazi spy. You have to tell me everything."

So I told Ruth the whole story, starting from when David and I overheard Schiendick talk about Operation Sunshine while we were feeding Peter. Ruth had a million questions and we almost missed lunch.

"I guess I wasn't a very good chaperone. Anyway, I'm proud of what you did."

We spent time after lunch packing and getting ready, once again, to leave the ship. All the passengers had been asked to let the purser know which of the four countries we wanted to go to: England, France, Belgium, or Holland. They told us every effort would be made to keep families together, but there were no guarantees. Each country had agreed to take a certain number of passengers.

Many people were so relieved not to go back to Germany, they were willing to go anywhere. Some, like the Jantzens, had family in one of the countries.

"I want to ask for England, where David's family's going," I told Ruth.

"England is fine. It'll probably be safer if there's a war, like people say might happen. And our parents will come, wherever they send us."

• • •

Friday afternoon David and I were on the deck. I couldn't stand to stay in my cabin any longer, and I felt pretty safe, having him with me.

"Look Hannah! Gulls!" David pointed. "We're nearing land."

We shared the binoculars, as always. While David had them trained on a high-flying gull, I noticed a couple of Schiendick's Gestapo crewmen stalking toward us across the deck. One of them was Schiendick's roommate! He pointed at me and said something to the other Nazi.

The Double Crossing

"David!" I pulled on his arm and pointed to the men. My mind replayed Schiendick dragging me onto the rail. These two together could just pick me up and toss me over.

Before the crewmen reached us, two other men cut them off. Pozner and another passenger. The four glared at each other menacingly, like dogs facing off, stiff legged, hackles raised. They talked back and forth in low voices. I heard a few words when they got louder: "Jew dogs!" from one of the crewmen and, "Report you to the captain," from Pozner.

Schiendick's men turned, glared at me again, and stamped away. Pozner smiled and waved at us before he and his friend ambled back across the deck.

I took a breath and wiped at the tears in my eyes. "Thanks for asking Pozner to help."

David held my hand until I stopped shaking.

• • •

On Saturday morning everyone was on the deck as the *St. Louis* approached the Dutch port of Vlissingen. Ruth and I stood with David's family, excited to see land again. Vlissingen was at the head of the large estuary we would follow to the Scheldt River and Antwerp, Belgium. There we'd all disembark and be transported to separate countries.

A tugboat approached the *St. Louis* and docked at the landing platform. Morris Troper, the man who had negotiated for us to be taken in by the four European countries, was on the boat. Sixteen other men, four from each of those countries, came with him. They would assign us all to our destinations.

I studied them anxiously as they climbed the accommodation ladder. These men would decide our futures.

Everyone crowded the rails, straining to see better. People tried to guess which countries the men represented. "How will they choose who goes where?" I heard a man ask.

A brief ceremony had been planned to thank Troper for saving our lives. It was Liesl Joseph's eleventh birthday, and her father was the head of the passenger committee, so she was chosen to give a welcome speech. She wore a frilly pink dress and shiny shoes with straps.

"I know Liesl," Rebekah said, standing on tiptoe for a better view.

When Mr. Troper stepped onto the ship, everyone applauded, then quieted as Liesl came forward and made a curtsy. In a clear voice she said, "We thank you with all our hearts. I am sorry that flowers do not grow on ships, otherwise we would have given you the largest and most beautiful bouquet ever." She smiled and stepped back.

"Your friend made a very good speech," Herr Jantzen whispered to Rebekah.

Captain Schroeder followed with another short speech to welcome and thank Mr. Troper. He asked Purser Mueller to guide them to the social hall to use as their office. There they would make their decisions as the *St. Louis* continued on her way to Antwerp.

• • •

"I heard the representatives of the four countries all prefer to take passengers who are on the waiting list to get into the U.S.," Herr Jantzen told us over lunch. "They want to get rid of us as soon as possible. Holland will only take those passengers, because they already have too many refugees from Germany."

"But there will be a place for everyone, won't there?" I suddenly lost my appetite. Ruth and I weren't on the list for the U.S.

"Don't worry. They've agreed to take us all. They're just scrapping over who gets to take the passengers who'll be leaving them soonest."

Once again, Jews weren't wanted. I clenched my teeth.

• • •

The Double Crossing

Just past two in the afternoon, we arrived in Antwerp. For the first time since leaving Hamburg, the ship was allowed to tie up at a dock. In the busy port, ships loaded and unloaded cargo and passengers, workers yelled back and forth, and people noisily greeted loved ones debarking from other ships.

The gangway was lowered. Police and customs agents boarded. A crowd of people waited on the quay. Some called out to passengers, friends and family members who must have heard the *St. Louis* was going to dock.

Leo joined me and David at the rail. "Good job, Hannah. What you did was very brave. A bit foolhardy, but brave."

I felt a glow of pride. "We all helped. I couldn't have done it without either of you."

"I hope Schiendick will be in hot water for failing his mission," Leo said. "Maybe the Nazis will lock him up and throw away the key. Otherwise, he's going to make trouble for me and the captain when we get back."

"Speaking of keys," David said. "What did the captain say? About the key? Was he mad?"

"He was pretty angry. He's taken away my shore leave."

"I'm sorry I made trouble for you," I said.

"Don't feel bad. I wish I could have helped more. Well, I wanted to say good-bye to you two and wish you luck. I might not have another chance. I'm going to be busy. We're behind schedule. We've got to provision the ship and be on our way. It's been great to know you."

"You too," I said, a sudden ache in my chest. This was good-bye? After all we'd been through together.

Leo shook David's hand warmly and then offered his hand to me. I smiled and reached out to take it.

"Be safe. Stay out of trouble." Leo turned and left us.

Tears came to my eyes as I watched our friend climb the stairs to the bridge deck. I hoped things would go well for Leo. I realized that once we left the ship, I'd probably never see him again.

39

MS *St. Louis*, Antwerp, Belgium
Saturday, June 17

DAVID

It felt like my world was coming to an end. Again. After all the ups and downs, all that we'd shared, everyone on the ship was about to go our separate ways. Saying good-bye to Leo left me feeling sad and empty. And now a claw gripped my stomach as I worried that Hannah and I might be separated.

I stood with her at the rail, watching the noisy activity of the port and waiting for the decisions being made in the social hall. Decisions that could determine the rest of our lives. My hand in hers couldn't keep us from being separated, but I held on tight.

Papa came toward us along the deck, walking stiffly and looking serious. Had he learned what country we'd been assigned to? It didn't look like good news.

"I'm glad you're both here," he said, his mouth tight and frowning. "I finally had a talk with the captain, and it wasn't about birds." His dark eyes sparked with anger as he glared at me.

That's what this was about. I turned to face him, fists clenched at my sides.

My father lowered his voice, still sounding tense. "He told me the two of you interfered with a Nazi spy operation."

The noise from the docks seemed to disappear and my vision narrowed. I glanced at Hannah.

She said, "Well, actually—"

"That's right, we did," I interrupted. "We stopped it. Are you mad at me?"

"Of course I am!" Papa raised his voice. "What were you thinking?"

A few people turned to look.

"Do you realize what could have happened to you?" He went on in a stern whisper. "Those are dangerous men. Why didn't you come to me for help?"

"We told Leo, then Captain Schroeder. But they couldn't go against the Party and the *Abwehr*."

"And the captain told you not to do anything!"

Although I was now almost as tall as my father, I felt small. What could I say? I couldn't meet his eyes. Looking down, I noticed Hannah was also staring at her feet and twisting her hands in her skirt.

"I'll admit what you did was very brave. But it was just luck you weren't killed. This was a problem for adults to handle."

"It was mostly my fault, sir," Hannah lifted her head to look at my father. "I didn't want to involve anyone else."

"Thank you, Hannah. But David was involved. It was a dangerous and foolish thing to do. Son, in the future I expect you to come to me and your mother with any serious problems like this."

"Yes, sir."

"Good. We'll leave it at that." He looked from me to Hannah and back, the stern expression still on his face. "We should have news from the social hall shortly." He turned and left us at the rail.

I watched him walk away and took Hannah's hand again. She was shaking.

"Don't worry," I said. "Your way worked out. You stopped Operation Sunshine. Maybe not as quietly as you'd hoped, but still, Papa wouldn't even have known about it if the captain hadn't told him."

• • •

Lists of the names of passengers going to each of the four countries finally went up in the social hall. People stood in front of them, talking excitedly, a few complaining or protesting.

I found my family's names on the list of 288 passengers assigned to England, as Papa had requested. I looked for Hannah's and Ruth's names without finding them on the list.

"Oh, here we are." Hannah's shoulders slumped. She pointed to the list of 224 passengers going to France. Other lists divided the rest of the passengers between Belgium and Holland.

"No!" I groaned, reading her name and Ruth's on the list for France. "Why? This can't be right."

She squeezed my hand.

I pulled her toward the table where the committee members sat. This had to be a mistake.

A clump of other passengers stood in front of the table, some loudly complaining and asking to have their assignments changed.

The committee members kept repeating the same response. "I'm sorry. We did the best we could. The quotas were strict. Assignments can't be changed without affecting someone else."

Hannah looked at me miserably. "There's no point in asking. The committee isn't going to budge."

We got separated in the crowd as we left the social hall. I found her again on deck where we went to find a quiet place.

"I guess I'll have to start …" Her voice broke and she wiped tears from her eyes, "start learning French."

She forced a small smile.

"You'll write to me, won't you?" I gently wiped away a tear under her eye with my thumb. "When you get somewhere? We'll stay in touch. And as soon as we can, we'll see each other again. Maybe the Nazis will be kicked out soon and I'll see you at home in Germany."

• • •

At five o'clock, Morris Troper announced over the loudspeaker that the passengers going to Belgium would eat a last dinner aboard the ship and disembark at seven that evening. "A special train will be waiting to take you to Brussels," he added.

A huge crowd gathered on the deck at seven to watch the group depart. People embraced and said tearful good-byes to friends they'd made on the voyage.

"They're lucky to be the first ones off the ship," a woman said.

"I can't wait to feel solid ground under my feet again," her friend replied.

Hannah and I watched, huddled together, dejected, saying nothing. Passengers bound for Belgium filed down the gangplank carrying luggage, holding small children by the hand, calling back and waving to friends on the ship.

The joy and excitement I'd felt about leaving the ship had evaporated now that I knew Hannah would be going to a different country. Anything could happen. Especially if war started.

At dinner, my family, even Rebekah, tried to cheer us up.

Papa said, "I'm sorry you won't be going to England with us, Hannah. I know that's what you and David wanted. But France is a beautiful country. They'll take good care of you and Ruth until your parents come. And just think, tomorrow we'll all be off to start a new life."

"Yes," said Mama. "I'll be so happy to be where water isn't rationed so we can wash clothes and take a bath again."

"Me too." Rebekah sniffed the sleeve of her blouse. "I'm starting to stink!"

We all laughed, but it didn't take long for the table to lapse into silence.

Sylvia Patience

• • •

At nine o'clock that evening all the passengers going to France were called on deck. I had a moment of panic, thinking Hannah would be leaving. But the announcement went on to say it was for them to be given identity cards.

I went with her. A man from the French consul came up the gangway. One by one, he handed each person a card stamped with words in French. People said they meant, "Refugee from the Saint Louis." Hannah and Ruth each received theirs. Hannah showed me hers.

"Look," she pointed. "This must be the French word. *Réfugié* isn't anything like our German word *Flüchtling*."

Each thing that happened now was moving us closer to good-bye. It wasn't fair. Especially for Hannah. She'd already been forced to leave her parents. Now they were taking her away from me and the friends she'd made on the *St. Louis*. There ought to be something I could do. Momentarily, I thought about talking to Captain Schroeder, asking him to make them send Hannah to England. But I knew the captain didn't have any say in where passengers were going.

"Are you okay?" I asked. She hadn't said much all evening.

She looked up at me, her eyes shiny with tears. But she wasn't crying. "If I could leave Mother and Father, and I could stop Schiendick's spy plan, I can do this." She straightened her back and raised her chin. That was Hannah.

40

MS *St. Louis*, Antwerp, Belgium
Sunday, June 18

HANNAH

I HADN'T SLEPT MUCH. Was it only a month since I'd had to leave Mother? And now David and his family.

I went to the dining saloon early for breakfast, but Ruth had gone even earlier to say good-bye to friends who were leaving for Holland. There wasn't much to be said for the food. Coffee or tea and porridge. Again. I pushed food into my mouth, hardly tasting anything, and went on deck.

Early morning light reflected on the still water of the river. A few cormorants stood on nearby pilings, their wings spread wide. The birds made me think of David. A small ship was tied up beside the *St. Louis*, waiting to take the passengers going to Holland. Farther along the deck, Ruth and three of her friends were hugging and saying good-bye.

I caught my breath when I saw David coming toward me. His blonde hair shone in the early morning light.

"I was saying good-bye to Aaron Pozner," he said. "He just boarded that boat to Holland. I sure hope he'll be able to send for his wife and children soon. He's had such a terrible time."

"I hope so too. I didn't get to talk to him much, but he helped you save my life."

"Have you heard?" David's face lit up. "The passengers for England and France are going on another ship together! That means we still have some time to … well … I don't know. Just time."

He gave me a foolish grin and reached for my hand. His cheeks were red and his eyes shining.

I smiled back. I forgot, for the moment, how sad and scared I'd been feeling. "No. I didn't know. That's great!"

"Hannah, you have my Aunt Retta's address. You can always write me there. Please write soon, so I'll know where you are and how to get in touch with you."

"I will. As soon as we get somewhere."

He took my hand. "Promise?"

I squeezed his hand.

"Of course! You're my best friend," I smiled up at him, "and more than that. And your family made me welcome. And …" I was blushing and suddenly felt tearful, "I don't know if I have anyone else, except Ruth. I'm worried about my parents."

"I hope you'll hear from them soon, with good news." He put his arms around me, and I leaned into him.

• • •

Early in the afternoon, the *Rhakotis* docked near the *St. Louis*. We'd been warned it wasn't as nice a ship. It was an old HAPAG freighter that had been quickly converted for passengers. There were no portholes, which meant no windows. But it would carry us the rest of the way. The *St. Louis* was going to sail directly back across the Atlantic to New York.

The *Rhakotis* would drop off everyone going to France in Boulogne. Then it would take David and all the others across the channel to Southampton, England.

At two o'clock we all began lining up on deck. I wished I could say a last farewell to Leo, and good-bye and thank you to Captain Schroeder. But they were busy on the bridge deck getting ready for the *St. Louis* to sail. I'd never see them again.

"Look!" David said in an excited whisper, pointing down at the gangway. "Isn't that Schiendick leaving the ship? He ended up needing that walking stick for more than hiding documents."

I couldn't fail to recognize Schiendick's broad back, even though he now walked with a limp and wore a suit and hat instead of his steward's uniform. He carried a large bag and leaned on the carved walking stick from Cuba.

"Good! Captain Schroeder won't have to put up with him anymore. I wonder what he'll tell the *Abwehr* about those papers."

"Probably not that a thirteen-year-old Jewish girl stole their top-secret documents and dumped them overboard." He smiled at me, a sparkle in his eyes.

Hearing it put that way made me pretty proud of myself.

Schiendick was followed by a few other crewmen, also out of uniform and carrying their bags.

"There go some of his Gestapo 'firemen' too," I said. "They must be returning to Hamburg. Good riddance!"

Each of us was handed a box lunch, with sandwiches and sweets. We'd been told to bring an overnight bag. Finally, after a month and five days on board the *St. Louis*, we walked down the ringing metal stairs of the gangplank with the remaining passengers and boarded the waiting cargo ship. Ruth and I stood at the rail of the *Rhakotis* with the Jantzens to watch the tugboats that were going to tow us upstream, where we'd spend the night at anchor.

"They say the Belgian authorities won't allow us to be docked near the *St. Louis* after four o'clock this afternoon," Herr Jantzen said. "For 'security reasons,' whatever that means. Our luggage will be left on the dock for us to pick up in the morning."

Two tugboats, one on either side of the old freighter, began pushing and tooting signals back and forth between each other and the ship as they moved her up the river.

"The boats are talking to each other, aren't they?" Rebekah said.

"That's right," answered her father. "I don't know what the signals mean, but that's how the captains communicate."

"I saw them do that in the harbor in Hamburg, when we used to go down to watch gulls," David said.

As we were towed up the river, ducks sprang into the air ahead of us. David didn't even lift his binoculars. He stared down at the water, frowning. I took his arm and stood close. Nearing the shore, I noticed two large birds with long, pointy bills facing off in the water. Reddish-orange feathers stood out like a ruff around their necks and they wore crowns of black feathers.

"See those birds?" I pointed. "What are they? Are they fighting? They're so odd looking."

David seemed to come back to himself. He aimed the binoculars.

"Oh! Grebes! Great Crested Grebes. Two males threatening each other. Here, look." He handed me the binoculars.

For a few minutes, our sadness was forgotten in watching the birds show off and charge at each other without an actual fight.

When the ship was in position, the tugboats chugged away and the *Rhakotis* anchored for the night.

I climbed down the ladder into the stuffy hold, glad we'd only have to spend two nights on board. Because the freighter didn't have enough cabin space for over five hundred passengers, HAPAG had converted the two windowless cargo holds into sleeping quarters by putting in rows of metal bunks, and long dining tables down the center. Women would sleep in the forward hold and men in the aft, with bathrooms on the deck.

Ruth and I claimed bunks together, me on top. Rebekah and Frau Jantzen took bunks next to ours.

Soon after we lay down to sleep, the air felt so suffocating I could hardly breathe. Ruth and I, and many of the other girls and women, pulled the thin mattresses off our bunks and hauled them on the deck to sleep in the fresh air.

All of us laid our mattresses down on the forward deck. Ruth flopped onto her bed.

"I'm too hot to go to sleep yet," I said. "I'm going to walk around in the air a while." Soon I caught sight of David at the rail.

"We're sleeping up here. There was no air down there with two hundred other men," he said.

"Same on the women's side. We're sleeping on the deck too."

It was around ten o'clock. The summer sunset painted the clouds and rising mist red and orange.

We stayed talking, savoring our little remaining time together, into the long twilight. David cleared his throat and shuffled his feet.

"What is it, David?" He always did this when he was embarrassed to say something.

He brought a little pair of scissors out of his pocket.

"I hoped I'd see you so I borrowed these from Mama. Would you let me cut a little piece of your hair? To remind me of you, until we see each other again?"

What a sweet idea. Tears came to my eyes. I smiled at him. "If I can have a piece of yours."

We made a ceremony of it, each snipping a lock from the back of the other's head and wrapping them in our handkerchiefs.

Around midnight, David pointed across the water. "Look—it's the *St. Louis!*"

The ship was slowly pulling away from the dock.

"They must be leaving for New York. I don't suppose we'll see the ship, or any of them, again."

"I hope the captain and Leo will be okay," he said. "Maybe it's a good thing they won't go back to Germany for a while. By then, Schiendick's complaints may be forgotten."

The Double Crossing

Many of the passengers on the *Rhakotis* were still up. We all watched silently as the *St. Louis* glided past. Her crew stood at the railings, waving and shouting, "Good luck to the Jews!"

David squeezed my hand. I wiped away tears. I hated endings. There'd been too many.

41

Rhakotis
Monday, June 19 – Tuesday, June 20

David

The tooting of boats' horns and motion of the freighter woke me. It took a moment to remember I was on the deck of the *Rhakotis*. We were being towed back to the dock to pick up our luggage where it had been unloaded from the St. Louis the night before.

I threw off my blanket and stood up. Blanket, deck, and the hair on my head were wet with dew. I rubbed my face and ran a hand through my damp hair to smooth it before going to look for Hannah. The dawn chorus of early morning birdsong barely caught my attention.

Hannah was up early too. I found her at the back of the ship, staring down at the water churning in our wake. For an instant, when she turned to me, she seemed lost, worry or despair in her eyes. Then she smiled.

"Good morning," we said at the same time.

The Double Crossing

I took her hand, and we watched the water, side by side, wrapped in silent misery. The boat tied up at the pier where the *St. Louis* had been docked, and the crew began hauling luggage on board.

Breakfast was served in the holds, so men and women ate separately. I walked Hannah to the forward hold, hating to lose any of our last day together.

"I'll meet you back on deck when you finish," I said, before she went down the ladder.

I sat with my father at the long table. The stuffy hold stank of men's bodies crowded together mixed with better smells of coffee, eggs, and sausages.

Papa ate heartily. "Isn't it wonderful to have eggs again? I believe it's been three weeks."

I didn't have much appetite. I couldn't stop thinking about Hannah, alone with only Ruth in France. What if she did something impulsive again, like trying to stop some other Nazi plot? What if she got into trouble, and I wasn't there to help her? I wouldn't even know about it.

I hurried through breakfast, went on deck and paced until Hannah joined me, after what seemed like forever. We spent the rest of the morning, while the ship remained at the dock, wondering about our futures and watching birds. The river was alive with them, swimming, flying, and wading: gulls, pelicans, herons, and several kinds of ducks.

"Hannah, don't forget to write to me right away, so I know where you are. And please be careful," I said, probably not for the first time.

"I will." She passed me the binoculars.

The morning seemed to fly by. I kept glancing at Hannah while she scanned the water with the binoculars or focused on a particular bird. How would she manage without any family? I couldn't concentrate on birds. I kept thinking, *This is our last day. It's not enough time.*

"Be careful," I said again. "Don't do anything dangerous. And write to me as soon as you get there."

"David, stop worrying." She lowered the binoculars and looked at me. "Ruth and I will be all right. And I will write you. As soon as I have an address. I promise"

"It's just that, I hate that we're going to different countries. Especially the way things are. There could be a war, you know."

"Yes, I know." Her eyes suddenly glistened with tears. She took a breath and forced a smile. "You know me. I'll be fine."

Morris Troper came on board the *Rhakotis* in the afternoon to say good-bye. He shook hands with each of the passenger committee members. We watched him go back down the gangway, get into a car and drive off. Everyone waved. People kept saying how he'd saved our lives.

I was grateful to the man, but if his negotiations had failed, if he hadn't been able to arrange a place for us to go, I knew Captain Schroeder would have carried out his plan to get us to England. The captain was a hero too, though almost no one knew it.

At last, the *Rhakotis* sailed, hugging the coast. Tomorrow morning in Boulogne, Hannah would leave with the other passengers bound for France, while my family would have to continue across the channel to Southampton, England.

Late in the afternoon, rain began pouring down. For a long while, Hannah and I still huddled together against a wall on the deck. Finally, both of us soaked and dripping, I let go of her hand and we returned to our separate holds for dinner. That night the storm forced all of us below to sleep in our bunks.

After tossing and turning in the suffocating dark, it felt as if I'd just fallen asleep when I woke to the sound of the anchor dropping. I went on deck, where the sky was beginning to lighten. It was four-thirty. The rain had stopped. We were anchored in the middle of a busy harbor, just like in Havana. This must be Boulogne. I hoped, unreasonably, that the French would have changed their minds, like the Cubans, and we'd all have to go to England.

The Double Crossing

In the grey light I saw docks and, beyond, what looked like a good-sized city still asleep. All I wanted to see was Hannah. After breakfast we found each other and stayed together on the deck. There was nowhere to be alone, but we stood close, whispering to each other.

At mid-morning, the passengers for France were separated from the others. Everyone was saying good-bye to friends made on the voyage. My parents and Rebekah hugged Hannah and wished her a safe trip.

I hugged her last. I took her hands, saying, "Don't forget—"

"I know, David. Don't worry. I'll write to you soon." Her eyes, green as the harbor in the morning light, held mine again.

It felt like a piece of me was being torn loose when Hannah slipped her fingers out of mine. Like when my family left our home in Hamburg for the last time. Worse. You don't always know when it's the last time you'll see someone.

I watched her in the crowd across the deck, standing next to Ruth. Each person in their group was handed a packed lunch before boarding a smaller boat which had tied up alongside the *Rhakotis*. Hannah waved from the deck as their boat's engine started and it began to chug away from us.

When I could no longer see her well, I watched through my binoculars until the boat arrived at the dock. My last sight of her was her red hair, glowing like a torch, as she walked down the gangway and disappeared in the crowd.

AFTERWORD

NEW YORK
1944

DAVID

M Y FAMILY ARRIVED in the United States over a year ago. I received no more letters from Hannah since the middle of 1940, after the German army invaded France. Before that, she'd written several times. For a while, I kept writing to the last address she sent, but she never answered.

Now, after so many years, a letter! Forwarded from my aunt in England nearly two months ago. On the upper left corner of the envelope was the name Hannah Coen and a return address in Maryland. I stared at it, stunned. It looked like her handwriting. It must be *my* Hannah. Here in the United States!

I still thought of her often, but without much hope of ever seeing her again. The news reported that Jews in France, Holland and Belgium were rounded up and deported to Germany after

The Double Crossing

the Nazis invaded. They were taken to concentration camps. I was afraid that's what happened to Hannah.

My family disembarked the *Rhakotis* in Southampton and went to live with Papa's sister. In September 1939, Germany and England declared war. By June 1940, after the battle of Dunkirk, everyone believed Germany was going to invade England next. German men in England, including Jews, were considered "enemy aliens," and put in internment camps. My father spent four months in a camp before he was released. Papa returned thin and pale, with stories of sleeping on the hard floor because there wasn't enough straw for mattresses.

Finally, in late 1942, our number came to the top of the waiting list to emigrate to the United States. Papa borrowed money from Aunt Retta and we crossed the Atlantic again, arriving in New York shortly after the New Year in 1943.

With shaking hands, I carefully tore open the envelope and read:

Dear David,

Forgive me for not writing for so long. I hope you still remember me as your friend. I doubt you got the few letters I sent after the occupation. If you did, I'm sure they were opened and censored.

After a few temporary placements, Ruth and I were sent to live with a generous and caring Jewish family in Bordeaux, in the south. That was around the time the German occupation began. What I couldn't tell you in my letters was that this family, and other members of their synagogue, helped many Jews flee France to escape the Germans. Bordeaux was the last station on the refugee's route to Spain and Portugal.

Then Bordeaux became a Nazi headquarters. They began rounding up Jews there and sending them to camps. Ruth and I, along with our hosts, had to flee. Over several difficult weeks, we made our way across the mountains into Spain and from there to Lisbon, Portugal. We spent over a year in that city until finally, with help from the Joint again, Ruth and I and several other refugees took a ship to the United States. Fortunately, we had some money to pay our passage from jewelry our mothers had sewn into our clothing. Their parting gift to us. This time, we were allowed to land.

One of the hardest things for me has been not hearing from my mother since the one brief letter I received in Cherbourg, on the St. Louis. Ruth hasn't had any word from her parents since we left Havana. Other refugees have told us that all the Jews who remained in Oldenburg were sent to camps. Mother would not have survived in such a place. I doubt Father ever returned from Sachsenhausen, where he was sent after Kristallnacht.

I tried several times to write you from Lisbon, but each time I picked up my pen, I was overcome by grief at the loss of my parents, and so many good people. I had no words.

Now, far from the war, I am at last beginning to accept the loss of my parents and to find my way back to myself.

I hope this letter finds you and your family well and safe in England. Give my love to your parents and dear Rebekah. I will never forget our time together on the St. Louis, our birds, and how you saved my life. Please write to me at this address. One day, God willing, we may see each other again and renew our friendship.

Your loving friend,
Hannah Coen

I read the letter several times. It was so long since I'd heard from her. I'd almost accepted that she was lost to me. Now here she was, and so near. I hoped she was still at the address on the letter, since it took months to get to me.

I was eighteen, working and taking college classes. I'd met other girls since Hannah, but no one like her. I remembered her determination and courage, her flaming hair and green eyes, sad or smiling.

I wiped away tears. Boys can cry too. Then I found stationery and a pen and sat down to write.

Author's Note

THE STORY OF THE *ST. LOUIS* IS TRUE. Most of the people and events in this book are taken from history. Almost everything in the story did happen. Hannah, David, and Ruth and their families are fictional characters, but their experiences in Oldenburg and Hamburg and on the *St. Louis* are based on things that happened to real Jewish families in those places.

At the time this story begins in May 1939, the Nazi government wanted the Jews out of Germany. They confiscated most of their possessions and money before letting them leave. But the German Propaganda Ministry intended to show the world that no one else wanted the Jewish people, in order to justify the Nazi's treatment of them. Anti-Jewish propaganda was stepped up in Cuba. Influential pro fascist Cubans contributed. By the time the *St. Louis* arrived in Havana, public sentiment had grown against allowing more Jewish refugees into the country.

The United States and Canada also refused to allow the refugees to land. Although there was much public sympathy for the plight of the passengers, there was also strong feeling that the U.S. should not take more than the quota of refugees it had already set.

Leo Jockl really was Captain Schroeder's steward. He was half Jewish. He told no one but the captain. When asked to investigate Schiendick's accusation that Leo was Jewish, Captain Schroeder cabled back that there was no evidence of it, just as he did in this story.

When he returned to Germany, Leo fell in love with an Aryan girl whose father was a Nazi official. Her mother denounced him as Jewish and they weren't allowed to marry, although they stayed together and had a child. He was drafted into a road gang of "half Jews" and killed in 1944 when an American fighter plane strafed the road.

Otto Schiendick and his Gestapo firemen did many of the things I've described. Schiendick was remembered as a bully. He was

The Double Crossing

a courier for the *Abwehr* and carried out his part of Operation Sunshine. Unfortunately, there was no Hannah Coen or David Jantzen to stop him. He delivered the secret documents about the U.S. military, which were smuggled to him in magazines and a walking stick by Robert Hoffman. He worked for the German secret service during the war until he was shot and killed in Hamburg by a British patrol in 1945, after a bombing raid.

Germany invaded Holland, Belgium, and France only months after the passengers left the *St. Louis*. Many passengers who were sent to those countries ended up in concentration camps. An estimated 250 of the 907 passengers who returned to Europe were murdered in those camps during the Holocaust. No one knows the exact number. Aaron Pozner was one of those. There is no record of what became of his wife and children.

Captain Schroeder commanded the *St. Louis* and ensured that his Jewish passengers were treated with respect. He was interested in birds. But as far as I know, he didn't make friends with any of the young passengers. He did form the desperate plan, which became unnecessary, to run the *St. Louis* aground, set her on fire, and evacuate the passengers in England, rather than take them back to Germany. After leaving the Jewish refugees in Antwerp, he continued his 1939 summer schedule until, in September, war was declared while he was returning across the Atlantic.

After Captain Schroeder got the *St. Louis* back to Hamburg, he never went back to sea. Shortly before his death in 1959, he received an award from the Federal Republic of Germany for his actions on the *St. Louis*. Much later he was given a posthumous award by the State of Israel. A street in Hamburg is named in his honor.

The *MS St. Louis* was heavily damaged by bombs in 1944. She was renovated and used as a hotel for a short time. In 1950, she was broken up for scrap.

Glossary

Aryan: Word used in Nazism to designate a supposed master race of non-Jewish Caucasians usually having Nordic features.

Mutter, Mutti: Mother

Liebling: Darling

ein Kopfkino: A head cinema or movie in the head

Vater, Vati: Father

Kristallnacht: The Night of Broken Glass. On the night of November 9-10, 1938, an attack against Jews and their establishments was carried out by Nazi officers and civilians across Germany.

Konzentrationslager: Concentration camp

Warteschlange: A long line like a snake

Schmutziger: Dirty

Jüde: Jew

Birnenkompott: Pear compote

Emil und die Detektive: Emil and the Detective, a 1929 German children's novel by Erich Kastner

Heil Hitler dir: "Hail Hitler to Thee", a favorite German Nazi song

Leiter: Leader

Nationalsozialisten: National Socialist or Nazi

Sei fein, nie fies: Be nice, never nasty

Liebe: Dear

Der Saukerl: The pig

Gestapo: Official secret state police in Nazi Germany

Abwehr: The military intelligence organization in Nazi Germany

Mein Gott!: My God!

Unglaublich!: Incredible!

Untermenschen: Subhuman

Ortsgruppenleiter: The chief Nazi of a group

Schlossgarten: The castle garden

Feiner Schmuck: Fine jewelry

Der kleine Scheisser: The little shit

Führer: Leader, the title used by Hitler

Apfelschorle: Carbonated mineral water and apple juice

Freut euch des Lebens: Rejoice in life

Diese Trottel: The chumps

Diese Schwein: The pigs

Deutsches Jungvolk: German youth or Hitler youth

Nein: No

Mörder: Murderer

Mannomann!: Boy oh boy!

Mein Kampf: My Fight. The name of Hitler's book about his life.

Dumm Juden: Stupid Jews

Wir dürfen nicht sterben: We must not die

Wir kommen nicht wieder: We will not return

Halt: Stop

Komm zurück: Come back

Zwielichtig: Lowlife

Jüdische Diebin: Jewish thief

Flüchtling: Refugee

Der Teufel: The Devil

Schutzstaffel: Also SS. Protection squadron, a major paramilitary organization under Hitler

Reich: Realm. The Nazi rule in Germany was called the Third Reich.

Resources

Voyage of the Damned by Gordon Thomas and Max Morgan-Witts is a day-by-day history of the voyage of the *MS St. Louis* and was a wealth of information in the writing of this book.

Alex's Wake by Martin Goldsmith was written by a grandson of one of the passengers. He reports on his grandparents' experience in Oldenburg upon the rise of the Nazis, the voyage of the St. Louis, and what followed for his grandfather and uncle in France.

Hitler Youth by Susan Campbell Bartoletti gives an excellent overview of the history of Hitler's rise and fall in Germany and the roles young people played.

"Die Panic Party," in *Die Marsbewohner sind da! Politische Satiren* (Mungo, Berlin: Carl Stephenson Verlag, 1939), pp. 50-62.

Online resources include:

- *Jewish Virtual Library*
- *The United States Holocaust Memorial Museum Online*

About the Author

Sylvia Patience has written two other books for middle grade readers: *Toto's Tale and True Chronicle of Oz*, the beloved Oz adventure retold from the point of view of Dorothy's little dog, and *The Weaver's Daughter*, which follows a young girl's immigration journey from Mexico. *The Weaver's Daughter* received a 2020 Moonbeam Children's Book award.

Several of Sylvia's short fairy tales have won prizes in the international Hans Christian Andersen contest in Sestri Levante, Italy, including first prize for a foreign entry in 2022. Her poems have appeared in *The Porter Gulch Review, Calyx Journal*, and poetry anthologies. Sylvia is a member of the Society of Children's Book Writers and Illustrators (SCBWI).

Sylvia lives in Santa Cruz, California with her family and small dog, where she enjoys seeing the variety of birds found along the coast, in the wetlands, and the mountains. You can find out more about her world and works at her website, *sylviapatience.com*.

Also by the Author

The Weaver's Daughter

Sometimes people disappear into the North and are never heard from again.

2020 Moonbeam Children's Award winner

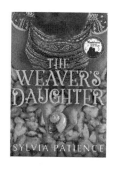

Available from Paper Angel Press in
hardcover, trade paperback, and digital editions
paperangelpress.com

You Might Also Enjoy

HAYCORN SMITH AND THE CASTLE GHOST
by John Kachuba

A boy is in danger when he stumbles upon a crime committed by two prominent men of his town, but finds an unusual ally in the form of a castle ghost.

Available from Paper Angel Press in
hardcover, trade paperback, and digital editions
paperangelpress.com

THE SMUGGLERS
FROM THE "TRUCK STOP AT THE CENTER OF THE GALAXY"
by Vanessa MacLaren-Wray

Attachment is everything.

Mother says, "Don't name the merchandise," and "Don't let the humans see you."

Available from Water Dragon Publishing in
hardcover, trade paperback, and digital editions
waterdragonpublishing.com

Made in the USA
Columbia, SC
24 October 2023

24624662R00157